A MURDER
ON
WALL STREET

A JOEY MANCUSO
FATHER O'BRIAN
CRIME MYSTERY
Book 1
BY
OWEN PARR

Title: A Murder on Wall Street
—A Joey Mancuso, Father O'Brian, Crime Mystery
Author: Owen Parr
Published by Owen Parr
owen@owenparr.com

ISBN 9781542693240

This is a work of fiction. Names, characters, businesses, places, events, and incidents are the products of the author's imagination or used in a fictitious manner. Any resemblance to actual persons, living or dead, or actual events is purely coincidental.

Dedication

To all law enforcement and first responder personnel.
Thank you for your dedication and unselfishness.

Quote

"Women are like police, they can have all the evidence in the world, but they still want a confession."

— *Melchor Lim*

Part One
CHAPTER ONE
Day 1
Tuesday

He jumped from the twenty-first floor of his office building? I thought after my brother texted me the news. I couldn't believe it.

This fellow who jumped—we called him Tito because Tito's vodka was his customary drink at our Irish pub and cigar bar— was celebrating last night with a stunning lady, a Marilyn Monroe look-alike. He bought French champagne for everyone and was headed to Portugal with her today.

I remember distinctly when Tito told me, "Joey, my life has changed for the better. I just landed a whale of an account for my firm. Life is good."

So, why would someone commit suicide after celebrating life the night before? After sixteen years as a homicide detective with the NYPD, I knew this didn't add up.

I'm Joey Mancuso, and my life has transformed in the last year. For sixteen years, since I was twenty, I went from a police cadet to a detective first-grade with the NYPD Homicide Unit. Last year, they forced me to take a disability pension or face some cooked-up charges by Internal Affairs. My record was impeccable, and my ratio of solved homicides was number one in Manhattan. However, it seems my methods, which had never been questioned before, were an excuse to boot me out of the force after my last case.

On my way to solving the murder of a homeless man in the alley of the famed 21 Club, I stepped on some dog shit, probably. The suspects involved were an up-and-coming politician and a Wall Street type with plenty of political juice. The NYPD *suits* made me an offer. Retire or face charges.

So here I am, half-owner of Captain O'Brian's Irish Pub and Cigar Bar on the corner of Hanover and Beaver Streets in Manhattan's Financial District. In 2016, my half-brother and the other half-owner of the pub, Father Dominic O'Brian, and I inherited the pub from his dad, Marine Master Sergeant O'Brian.

Father Dom is not your typical Irish priest. Yes, he is dedicated to his flock and his duties as a priest. But like me, he is unconventional in his ways. Fifteen years my elder, he was my mentor, my moral compass, and my substitute father. Every day, Dom takes time from his busy schedule to stop in at the bar and help in any way he can. If he were not a Catholic priest, he would be a skilled detective as he loves solving crime mysteries. Dom's demeanor could be mistaken for someone who was always serious. Those that know him know better. Reserved but affable. He is tall, thin, and good-looking. Blue piercing eyes and reddish hair.

My cell phone rang. The caller ID showed Dom's picture.

"Hey, how ya doing?" I spoke.

"Joey, are you watching the news?" Dom asked.

Normally, our flat screens are on sports channels. Today, I had one on a news channel. "Yes, I saw a commotion two blocks away. Lots of police and first responders, so I'm watching."

"Can you believe who jumped to his death?" Dominic queried.

"I can't. Our Tito. I heard his name is, or was, Jonathan something."

Dom went on, "I'm not buying the suicide line. I mean, I was there last night when he was celebrating his new account. No way he was depressed like they are saying. To jump from a twenty-first-floor window? Don't you agree?"

"You may be right," I said and added in my non-PC manner, "the only reason to commit suicide is if the big-breasted platinum blonde with the tight red halter top he was with told him it was over last night."

Father Dom didn't react to my humor. "Let's follow up on this. I think we may have a case to research if it's ruled a suicide. I'll be in later."

I hung up. Hearing the traffic from the busy street that fronted our bar was always the clue that someone was entering our establishment. I turned to see who had walked in. It was Marcela. FBI Special Agent Marcela Martinez, or Marcy, for short. Here was a striking Cuban bombshell—a body that left nothing to the imagination, bright and big green eyes that could mesmerize anyone, and long, thick auburn hair that she usually wore in a ponytail. When she let it loose, wow, I could feel a tingling up my legs. She was wearing a newly FBI-issued sidearm, a forty-caliber Glock 22 on her left side, and a gold shield on her right. She was hot. We had discussed marriage at one time, but the two of us being in law enforcement put a strain on our relationship. So, we had decided...make that she chilled and let things take their course for a while. Still, when I saw her, my heart responded with palpitations. I fell hard for her two years ago, and I wanted nothing else but to settle down with her. However, Marcy was cautious, and frankly, I had given her reasons to feel that way.

"Marcy, good afternoon. What brings you here?" I said, smiling.

"Hey, lover. Hi, Mr. Pat," she replied, waving at Mr. Pat, who was behind the bar stacking glasses on the shelves. "I was two blocks away at the scene of the jumper. Did you hear about that?"

I pointed to the television. "Watching it now. Why were you there? They're saying it's suicide."

Marcy replied, "You know. The Bureau's White-Collar Crime Division wanted someone there since this guy is a Wall Streeter. Though, there seems to be nothing for me to do there. So, here I am."

"Marcy, can I get you your usual?" Mr. Pat asked.

"That would be great, Mr. Pat. Thank you. Lots of ice, please," she replied.

"One Pellegrino rocks coming up," Mr. Pat said.

Patrick O'Sullivan. We called him Mr. Pat. Had served with Dom's father, Marine Master Sergeant Brandon O'Brian, in Vietnam. Returning together from the war, Mr. Pat worked alongside Dom's father since he took over the pub from his dad, Captain Sean O'Brian. Mr. Pat was a large man with red curly hair and a full red beard. He spoke English perfectly, but he preferred using an Irish brogue. He always said it added a certain authenticity to the pub.

"Have a seat," I said, pointing to a comfy captain's chair at the table where I was sat. "The guy who jumped? We call him Tito. He was here yesterday celebrating a new account he had just gotten. He was happy as a pig in mud."

"Really? His name is Jonathan Parker. He was a senior VP of his firm. So, what are you saying?" Marcy asked.

"I don't know. Father Dom seems to think it wasn't a suicide. We took care of this guy while he was here. I mean, he was buying French champagne for everyone. Had a trip planned for Portugal with his hot squeeze."

"So, you noticed she was a hot squeeze?" she wisecracked.

I turned to Patrick. "Mr. Pat, help me out here. Was this guy's lady a hot squeeze or what?"

Marcy turned to Mr. Pat and smiled.

"I was tending bar at the other end. I know nothing," Mr. Pat replied in his Irish brogue and with his eyes opened wide.

I added, "Even Father Dom was a little apprehensive. I mean, she was wearing a very tight red halter top, and her—"

Marcy interrupted, "Fine, fine. I don't need you to paint a picture. I'll monitor the last report and let you know."

"Who did he work for?" I asked, opening my hands.

"Evans, Albert, and Associates. A hedge fund."

"Evans? Isn't Evans a big political donor?" I asked.

"Darling, many Wall Streeters are big political donors."

"Can you find out who the..." I hesitated, "the lady was?" I asked, not wanting to share some information I already had on 'halter top.'

"Oh? So, now she's a lady. Not a hot squeeze?"

"We had a unique name for her."

"Do all your customers have nicknames?"

"We never ask a customer their name. That's a rule of mine. If they volunteer their name, that's fine. Otherwise, yes, we name them usually based on their drink of choice. However, this lady earned a unique name, 'cause—"

Marcy put a handout. "I don't want to hear it."

I stood to stretch my bad knee. "I was kidding. Father Dom thinks there is more to this than meets the eye, and I agree with him."

"I guess it can't hurt. I'll let you know once I get back to the office. Bye, Mr. Pat," she said as she turned to leave the bar.

"Bye, Marcy. Be good," replied Mr. Pat.

"Only if I have to, Mr. Pat," Marcy joked.

"What? No kiss?" I asked.

Without turning, Marcy waved back at me and said nothing. She pushed down the Glock holster on her waist.

I love spunky women with attitudes.

CHAPTER TWO
Day 2
Wednesday

Our research lay strewn over the bar. We don't open the pub until two in the afternoon. During morning hours, we use the bar to brainstorm any cases we are working on. So, here we were. Developing a case file for what Father Dom baptized the "Murder on Wall Street."

Dom was in early today. His church duties for the morning had been completed. Now, he was ready to jump on this. Of course, we didn't know if, in fact, we had a case. That's how most of our investigations began...with a hunch.

The night before, Father Dom had compiled a case file with some of the potential suspects on his computer at St. Helen's Rectory in Brooklyn.

"Joey, this is a picture of Robert Evans, co-owner of Evans, Albert, and Associates. Mr. Evans is fifty-eight. Married with two children. His son, Robert Jr., is married and working as an attorney in Chicago. The daughter, Stephanie, is attending NYU studying for her law degree," said Dom.

He displayed photos of the family he had printed from social media on the bar.

"Don't we have enough attorneys already?" I said.

Dom didn't respond, showing more pictures. Then added, "Here is Thomas Albert III. Also, partner and co-owner of the firm. Married to Lillian. Three children. He's sixty. Before opening the hedge fund with Evans, they both worked at Salomon Brothers as bond traders."

"I remember reading a book that said these bond traders at Salomon called themselves 'the big swinging dicks'," I said.

"You *would* remember that," Dom said, in a somewhat disapproving tone.

"What else you got?"

"Moving on, the last person I researched is Mrs. Jonathan Parker. Adelle."

"Wait, a second. Tito, or Jonathan Parker, was married?"

"Yes, to his wife of eight years. Here's her picture."

"So, *'Miss Big Breast'* was a plaything? There you go. The wife did it." Eyeing the picture, "Wow, an attractive lady. Do they have kids?"

"No, no children."

"My hunch was right. Tito was paying for—"

Dom quipped, "Don't say it."

"I was going to say paying her rent. That's all."

Mr. Pat came into the bar. "Working on the case, boys?"

"It's promising. We might have something here. We have a wife, a mistress, and two senior partners who were part of a group who called themselves 'the big swinging dicks.' What do you think, Mr. Pat?"

Patrick laughed. "I'd be careful with those guys. Who wants a macchiato? I'm making myself one."

Dom passed, but I replied, "Perfect timing. I was going to light a cigar."

I'll get it for you. Rocky Patel 1999 Vintage?" Patrick asked.

"Yes, a Churchill, please, Patrick. Thanks."

Dom said, "I'm going to call Evans and Albert to see if I can stop by and ask a few questions. Joey, why don't you take Mrs. Parker and find more about the young lady from last night. Try to meet with them."

"Happy to do so. But what is our reason to do this? The police are calling this a suicide."

"Has it, in fact, been ruled a suicide?" Dom asked.

"I'll call Marcy and see if it has. But we still need a reason to speak to these people, don't we?"

"We are licensed private investigators, aren't we?"

"Yes, but who is the client?" I asked.

"Key word is private. We never divulge who the client is."

"Let me call Marcy," I said.

Dom added, "Let's find out if there is a life insurance policy on this guy. Perhaps the life insurance company might want to hire us."

I smiled and nodded as Marcy answered her phone. "Marcy, it's me."

"I can see that. I still have that idiotic picture of you on my cell phone's contact list."

"Hey, don't forget. You were next to me in bed when I took that selfie."

"Yeah, well, I need to delete it. What do you want?"

"That hurts my feelings."

"I'm sure. What's up?"

"Has the Parker death been ruled an official suicide?" I inquired.

"You guys on that?"

I walked behind the bar to get a glass of water. "Father Dom, through his divine intervention, has a hunch. We have nothing else going, so, yes, we're considering it."

"Who is your client?"

"Ah, we don't have one yet. We're working on that, too."

"I see. The body is still at the morgue. They ruled his death a suicide at the scene, so there is no rush for the medical examiner to do an autopsy."

"But, in New York, a suicide requires an autopsy, right?"

"That's why the body is with the ME, Mr. PI."

"You want to join me and pay a visit to the ME's office?"

"No, I have no reason to. The FBI isn't involved."

"What if this was a crime involving the partners covering something up?"

"You have any proof of that?"

"What if I get some?"

"At that point, you can call me and let me know. In the meantime, I don't want you dragging me into this. Mancuso, don't use my name at the coroner's office, either. I don't need my boss all over my ass again."

"If your boss gets close to your ass, you tell me. I'll take care of him," I replied. Father Dom sat wide-eyed.

"My boss is a woman."

"In that case, let me know, and I'll join you both."

"You are a sick puppy. Bye, Joey," Marcy said, clicking off her phone.

Father Dom turned to face me and asked, "Are they doing an autopsy?"

"In time. They don't seem to be in a hurry. I'll stop by the ME's office tomorrow. I know all those people there."

"Where are we going to start?" Dom asked.

"We have a bar to tend to. I'll call what's her name and ask her to stop in this evening."

"Who is that?"

"The mistress," I answered.

"How did you get her name and number so fast?" Dom asked, a bit dumbfounded.

"I follow your teachings, Bro. Ask, and you shall receive."

"You got her number when she was here?"

"When the jumper was making the rounds around the tables serving the champagne he bought, she asked if I was hooked up with anyone."

"To which you answered, 'no, I'm not'?"

"Not exactly. When she wrote her first name and number on a napkin, I filed it in the cash register."

"I don't think even if I became the Pope that God would save your soul, my little brother."

"Father, you better intercede for me."

It was my turn to talk to the big-breasted red halter top. Reaching into the cash register, I retrieved the napkin with her number.

After a few minutes on the phone with her, I had more information.

Her name was Melody Wright. She was an aspiring actress working as a model. She lived on UWS, which is the acronym for the affluent area of the Upper West Side. Donald Trump built her apartment complex named Riverside South. For an aspiring actress and part-time model, in my opinion, the rent was beyond her capabilities. Unless, of course, she was the recipient of a nice inheritance. Or maybe our jumper, Tito, was footing the bill.

She was more than happy to stop by the pub later in the evening.

CHAPTER THREE
Day 2

There was a thin lingering grayish-white cloud of cigar smoke that rose from the patron's seats as it reached the mid-level of the pub and then disappeared into the ceiling. The sound of clinking glasses, the occasional outburst of laughter, and the constant buzz of conversation pervaded the establishment. We always had music playing. Our choices were the old favorites. This evening, the voice of Frank Sinatra in the background softly permeated the pub. Our regulars loved singing along with Sinatra's 'New York, New York' every time it played. The aroma of cigars, scotch, gin, and other fine spirits infused the atmosphere. Somehow, it all blended quite nicely. Our pub enjoyed a life of its own.

Father Dominic's grandfather, U.S. Marine Captain Sean O'Brian, established Captain O'Brian's Pub and Cigar in 1948, upon his return from World War Two. The pub was a family institution in the Financial District of Manhattan. It catered to military and police personnel, as well as Wall Street types and other questionable clientele.

The bar was busy. Our usual Wall Street crowd was here. The stock market had a record up day. All the Wall Streeters, both gents and ladies, were celebrating, sitting towards the back, lighting up the cigars, and enjoying their single malts. These folks drank for any occasion. When the stock market took a dump, they would drink to drown their sorrows. Although, some made lots of money on those days, too. It was when the markets had a flat day that they would go home early. No action meant no transactions; one regular had explained. Our other patrons, an eclectic group of police and unsavory characters, were latecomers to the bar. It almost seemed like there was a second shift. Wall Streeters would leave, and the new characters would come in. It worked just fine for us. The second shift was more beer and well drinks, as opposed to the premium liquor of the first shift.

Around six in the evening, I heard the crowd go quiet for a minute. Sure enough, Melody had just walked in. As she walked towards the back, I could see that she was in mourning. At least, she was wearing black—a tight black skirt that outlined her well-formed and rather large derriere with a matching white silk blouse. The blouse was tight with a revealing cleavage somewhat disguised with a black silk scarf.

Everyone in the place followed her every step. I walked towards her to fend off the admiring crowd. As I approached her and gently put my arm around her waist, there was a collective sigh and some boos from my patrons.

She smiled softly, staring into my eyes, and I nodded towards the back of the bar. I could hear a few people say, "Mancusooo, Mancusooo." A bunch of pigs, these guys are.

"Are you taking me to the confessional booth?" Melody asked in a California girl intonation in which they always finish a sentence with a high-pitched tone.

"You've heard about that," I replied. "It's private. We can talk there. I remember what you drank last night. Can I get you a Cosmo?"

"No, how about a Manhattan?"

"A Manhattan, of course. Have a seat, and I'll be right back," I replied. I walked to the bar and asked Mr. Pat to get us the drinks.

Father Dom came over to our booth and said, "Ms. Wright, I'm sorry to hear about Mr. Parker."

"Thank you, Father. That's very nice of you."

"If there is anything I can do—" Dom began.

I interjected, "I've got this, Father."

"Yes, of course you do," said Dom, a little perturbed at my interruption. "I'll leave you two."

"Thank you again," Melody said, smiling at the good father. "So, Joey, tell me about this picture of Woody Allen and this man," she said, pointing to a black-and-white picture of Woody Allen and Dom's father over the booth.

"We also call this the Woody Allen Booth. He used to frequent the pub and sat back here, mostly by himself, when he wanted to be alone."

"Oh, my God, that's so interesting," she mused.

I added, "The black and white photos over the green glass shaded banker's lamps on the walls above the booths are a pleasant touch. What we gathered here is a history with these memories. Father Dom's grandfather, Captain Sean himself, with Norman Mailer, Truman Capote, and Babe Ruth. Goes back so many years. Then, there is Dom's dad, Brandon, with Broadway Joe Namath, The Mick—Mickey Mantle."

"So, when I become famous, will you put up my picture?"

I smiled, "Of course, I will," I said, smiling. "Let me get back to the reason I asked you to stop by. Tell me, how are you feeling?" I asked in a hush.

"This is devastating. I loved him so much, and we were going on a trip today," she said, pushing her platinum blonde hair back from her face with both hands.

"To Portugal, I think, right?"

"Yes, to Lisbon and on to Madrid."

"Do you mind if I ask you a few questions?"

"Are you still a detective? Jonathan mentioned you were or had been with the NYPD."

"No, I'm not with the force anymore. I'm retired. I am curious, though."

Our drinks came, and I thanked Angela, the server.

"Is there any reason you can think of why Jonathan would have committed suicide?"

"Oh, my God. You're thinking what I'm thinking."

"What is that?"

"So, why would he commit suicide if we were going on a trip to celebrate?"

I hate when everyone starts his or her sentences with the word *'So.'* Just drives me insane. "Celebrate the new account?" I asked.

"Not just the new account. We were getting engaged in Lisbon."

"I have to ask this. Did you know he was married?"

"So, yeah, to that bitch, Adelle. But he was dumping her soon."

"He was?"

"We were getting engaged. It's not like he can have two wives, right?"

"Right, of course. How soon was the marriage or divorce going to happen?"

"So, he wanted to be married before we went to Aspen for New Year's and celebrated our honeymoon there."

If I hear one more *'so,'* I swear, I'm going to kill myself. "Got it. That would make it in the next six months?"

"Yes, depending on the divorce."

"Did his wife know about the divorce? Before you answer that, I need a favor."

"What is it?" she said, smiling.

"You know I'm Italian?"

"Mancuso is Italian, yes."

I did a rapid survey of the premises to make sure no one was listening. "In Italian, the word *'so'* is a dirty word, and while nothing really offends me, there might be others who are troubled when they hear that."

"Oh, my God. I did not know. I am so sorry."

"That's another thing. Try not to use 'oh, my God' as often. Father Dominic is sensitive when people use those words in vain."

"Of course, of course. What was your question?" Melody asked, taking a sip of her Manhattan.

"The divorce...was Mrs. Parker aware?"

"Jonathan hadn't told her. He was planning on doing it after we came back from Madrid."

"I see. You both had the wedding planned, but Mrs. Parker was unaware."

"That's what Jonathan had planned, yes."

"What if Mrs. Parker contested the divorce? Sometimes, it takes a while to settle those things."

"They weren't getting along. I think Jonathan suspected she was playing around on him."

"Did he?"

"He never came out and told me, but I know he had more than an inkling."

This was getting interesting. I looked around before I asked, "Let me ask you this. You think someone pushed him out a window?"

"Oh, boy. Maybe, it was his wife or her father?"

"Why would you think that?" I questioned.

"He was having issues with her. Serious ones. Her father was very upset at something going on in the office. I don't know what, but they had heated arguments, occasionally."

"Would you like another drink?"

"Are you trying to get me drunk?"

I smiled, "No. Somehow, I think it takes over two drinks to get you drunk." I nodded to the server and made a circling sign with my index finger to do another round.

"You know, Joey, I find you attractive. I love your jet-black hair combed back like that and your rugged face with that tough-looking jaw. I bet you boxed when you were younger."

"Why? Because my nose is crooked?"

"It's actually a sensual nose," she replied, smiling."

"My nose?"

"Yes. And the rest of your face is rugged. Manly. A man's man. And, your nose, like I said, sensual."

I had never heard that before. "Thank you, it never got fixed after I broke it. I'll remember that."

"I hope you do," she said, reaching over with her shoeless feet and rubbing my legs.

"Couple more questions if you don't mind," I said, trying to concentrate on the matter at hand.

"You really sound like a cop."

"Once a cop, always a cop, right? Sixteen years solving crimes, it's become a habit."

"Go ahead. What else you want to know?"

Our drinks came, and I waited for Angela to serve her Manhattan and my Brooklyn Lager.

"What happens to you now?"

Tears developed in her eyes. "I don't know. My life is ruined."

"Do you work? Do you have income?"

"Why? You think I was a kept woman?"

"I don't know. I don't mean that as an insult."

"I've been fortunate. I have money put away, and yes, Jonathan helped with the apartment. But I didn't need his help. He just wanted to do it."

My hunch was correct. Jonathan was footing the bill for the apartment. "I see. Was he a wealthy man?"

"I suppose, never asked that. He spent it like he had it. And he was going to earn a lot more now that he'd become a partner."

"He was going to become a partner at his firm?"

"Yes, the new account meant that much to his company. We were going to be so happy," she said as a fresh wave of tears emanated from her eyes.

I reached for my handkerchief and handed it to her.

"Thank you, you are one of the few remaining gentlemen that carry a handkerchief."

"My father made sure I always carried one," I said. I never knew why he had done that.

"What are you going to do now?" I asked.

"So...oops, I'm sorry. I said the word."

"It's okay. Go on."

"Life goes on. Modeling and acting. Mr. Evans called—that's one of Jonathan's senior partners at the firm—and he said he knew a producer who was putting together this off-Broadway play and was looking for fresh faces. Maybe, I'll follow up on that. That is my dream, you know."

Evans called. How curious. "Good, good. When did you meet this fellow, Evans?"

"Jonathan had poker night once a month in my apartment. Mr. Evans came once to play."

"Have you ever seen him again?" I asked, taking a sip from my beer.

"What are you asking?" she asked, a bit rattled.

"Just that. Have you seen him again?"

"No, never seen him since that first time," she replied, glancing down at her drink.

"But he knew you were an aspiring actress?"

"Jonathan told him that when we first met."

"I see."

"Can you answer a couple of questions for me?" she said, smiling and downing her Manhattan.

I guessed I should reciprocate, so I said, "What's on your mind?"

"It's personal, but I'm curious about your father and family."

"Oh, no problem. Father Dom and I share a mother. Her name is Briana."

"Does she live in New York?"

"No, she's retired in Florida."

"What about your dad?"

"My dad was second-generation Italian from Brooklyn. He followed my grandfather's lifestyle and career."

"Which is?"

"Was. Dad passed away in a shooting at a bar in Little Italy a few years ago." I added, "*La mela non cade lontano dall'albero.*"

Melody snapped back her head. "Excuse me. What was that?"

"The acorn doesn't fall far from the tree. My dad followed his dad in the family business, and I was headed that way, as well." I loved my dad, and my memories of him were good growing up in Brooklyn. His lifestyle was another story, but he never exposed his *famiglia* to the dangers associated with his chosen profession.

Melody spoke, bringing me back to the present. "So, what happened? How come you didn't?" she asked, again moving her shoeless feet now up to my groin area.

I had to stop the conversation. "God sent Father Dominic to intercede on my behalf. He literally pulled me out of that lifestyle."

"Good for Father Dom. I really like him."

"Melody, I'm going to have to get back to the bar."

"What happens now?" she asked as she had aggravated my reaction to her feet. She realized she had and chuckled.

"What do you mean?"

"You and me. Can we get together?" she whispered her question with a mischievous glance at the pub. So much for the grieving mistress.

"Maybe, after you're done with your mourning. We can get together for a drink again."

"I was thinking more than a drink. How about your office? Now?"

CHAPTER FOUR
Day 3
Thursday

Father Dominic had made an appointment to speak to both Evans and Albert after his church duties in the morning. He stopped by the bar just before walking over to the office building where their offices were.

"Mr. Pat, you are always first in, last out," Dominic said.

"This place is my life, Father. You know that. I feel at home here with all the memories of your father."

"Yes, I know, but you need to have a life outside these walls."

"I've had a good life, and I've experienced a lot of things. Helping you guys here is of great satisfaction. Trust me."

"We love having you here. Any word from Joey?"

"He was headed to the ME's office this morning. After that, he was to visit the wife of the gentleman that jumped."

"I left before he..." pausing, he added, "finished talking to Ms. Wright. Did he say anything related to the case about her to you?"

"He said he didn't see a motive on her end to be implicated in any foul play. That's all he told me about the case. He asked that you call him before going over to the Evans and Albert offices."

"Thank you. I'm headed over to their office to speak to both partners. I'll be back afterwards. I'll call Joey on the cell on my way there."

"I'll be here. You take care of business, Father."

Father Dominic called Joey and walked the two blocks to the office building. It was a warm morning in the city. There was still a yellow tape under the second-story landing that protruded from the building. Evidently, Mr. Parker had landed there. Not on the sidewalk. Father Dominic glanced from the sidewalk towards the top of the building, imagining the flight this fellow took. The glare from the sun blinded him, and he squinted to focus on the windows of the floor he assumed Parker jumped from.

Taking the elevator and pushing the button marked 21, he removed his white collar from his neck, not wanting to use his priestly attire when he was involved with non-clerical activities. He still wore his black shirt and black pants, but he added a gray blazer. This gave him the appearance of a mid-level executive wearing casual Friday clothes.

Approaching the receptionist, he said, "Good morning, I'm Dominic O'Brian. I have an appointment with Mr. Evans and Mr. Albert."

"Yes, Mr. Dominic. Have a seat. I'll let them know you're here."

Sitting in a plush waiting area, he eyed the walls. Paneled with mahogany wood that went for a width of about ten feet, alternating with light blue silk wallpaper. Brownish marbled floors with gold veins covered the floor, along with thick area rugs with a darker blue tone matching the wallpaper. Mahogany baseboards and crown moldings framed the walls. Everything about the offices depicted high net worth. Yet, it was subdued. Nothing flashy or boorish.

"Father Dominic, how good to see you," said a young lady as she approached to take him back to a conference room.

Father Dominic raised his head quickly, surprised that someone knew he was a priest. "Stella, no, wait. Kathy, how are you? I didn't know you worked here."

"Yes, I am...or was Mr. Parker's assistant," she said, lowering her head.

"Oh, I'm so sorry, Kathy."

"Follow me. They're waiting for you."

As he walked to the conference room, Father Dominic noticed that, while the building was old, they had completely renovated it to stay relevant to the newer high rises in the area. The windows, he observed, were still the old type that could be opened out and sideways. When he walked into the conference room, both Evans and Albert stood to greet him.

Kathy said, "Father, can I get you some coffee or water?"

The partners exchanged a glance as they extended a handshake.

"Coffee would be great, Kathy. Cream, no sugar, thank you," Dom replied as he walked over to shake hands with the partners. Kathy nodded and walked out.

"Good morning, Mr. O'Brian, or is it Father O'Brian?" Evans said in a high-pitched voice.

Shaking hands with both, Dom smiled as Evans pointed to a seat at the conference table. "Please, call me Dominic, but, yes, I am a priest," He replied. Dom noticed Evans looked thinner and older than the picture he had previewed on the social media page. Evans was a small, short person, around five feet seven inches at most, with beady brown eyes and a blonde toupee.

"Kathy attends your church?" Albert asked in a raspy-toned voice. Albert, unlike Evans, was a tall and hefty individual. He was bald on the top of his head but had long stringy white hair down to his collar. Dom could see that both ears had been pierced at one point.

Dom smiled and thought to himself that he was looking at an older version of the comedy duo of Penn and Teller. "No, she's a patron at a bar I own with my brother two blocks from here."

"Wait. Is it Captain O'Brian's?" Evans asked.

"The same, yes," replied Dom.

"Never would have guessed. How did you end up being a proprietor of a bar?" Albert questioned.

"Long story short, my brother and I inherited the business from my father, who inherited the business from my grandfather."

Evans smiled. "Was he *the* Captain O'Brian?"

"That was my grandfather. He opened the bar after the Second World War years ago."

"Your place is an institution, Father. I'm thrilled to meet you. What brings you here?" Evans asked.

"I wanted to ask you a few questions about the late Mr. Jonathan Parker."

Both partners exchanged glances again. Almost in unison, they moved closer to the table and leaned toward Father Dom.

"Happy to discuss, but what interest is it to you? Was Parker a member of your church?" Albert asked.

"He was also a patron of the bar, but no, not associated with my church."

Evans covered his mouth with his right hand and pressed his thumb on his cheek. He said, "I still don't understand your involvement in Jonathan's unfortunate suicide."

Father Dom noticed the gesture.

"Do you follow up on every patron of your bar that has an accident?" Albert asked as he adjusted his position in his chair.

"Let me explain. Besides being the owner of a bar with my brother, we are both licensed private investigators and—"

"Excuse me," Evans said, cutting Dom short. "You are a priest, an owner of a bar, and a private investigator?"

"Yes, that's correct. When my brother retired from the NYPD, we both became PIs. It's just something we enjoy doing," Dominic replied.

Albert sat back in his chair. "Do you, also, carry a gun, Father?" he said, laughing, as Evans mirrored his movement and sat back.

"No, no guns. We have no need for that in our work," responded Dom, crossing his legs and adjusting the crease on his pants.

Kathy walked in with Father Dom's coffee, and the conversation halted momentarily. She looked at Dom as she placed the coffee on the conference table but avoided the partners.

"Why are you investigating a suicide?" Evans inquired once Kathy walked out.

"I wouldn't call it an investigation. We're simply trying to clear up some questions."

Albert leaned forward, placing his open arms on the table, and asked, "And, just who is your client?"

"They want to remain private," replied Dom.

"Go ahead, then. Ask your questions," said Albert, glancing at Evans.

"Thank you. How long did Mr. Parker work here?"

"He's been with us, what? About four years," replied Albert. Evans nodded.

"I understand he was about to become a senior partner because of a new account he landed. Is that correct?"

"Ah, we call those clients 'whales.' Yes, he landed a whale. In fact, he was being considered for a senior partnership role," Albert replied.

"Why would someone about to reap huge rewards for his work, and was celebrating the night before, jump to his death?"

Evans sat up and placed his arms on the conference table. Clenching his fists, he replied, "We are both as dumbfounded as you are, Father. He had a brilliant future with us."

"Perhaps ask his wife and father-in-law. They were both here just before he jumped. I have a feeling there was something not quite right with their marriage," added Albert.

Evans quipped, turning to glance at Dominic, "Well, the gambling may have had something to do with it."

"Did he gamble a lot?" Dom asked.

"From what we know. Poker, horse races, and all the football and basketball games," Albert said.

"Enough to commit suicide?" Dom asked.

Evans replied smiling, "You're the investigator, Father."

"You mentioned Mrs. Parker and her father were here. They were both here just before he jumped?" Dom questioned.

"Yes, and there was a heated argument we overheard. We didn't see them when they left, but I heard Mrs. Parker left first. Her father remained behind for a few minutes," Evans replied.

"Was it immediately before he jumped?" Dom asked.

Evans asked, "Oh, I see where you're going with this. You're asking if they pushed him out the window?"

"We don't know that. Possibly. They did not discover his body immediately after he jumped," began Albert. "He landed on a second-floor landing that goes the length of the building in the front. It extends over the sidewalk, and no one noticed when he landed on it."

"Did any of you see him after Mrs. Parker and her father left?"

Glancing at Evans, Albert moved forward in his seat and said, "No, we did not."

"Okay. Was there a suicide note found?"

Evans replied, "None that we are aware of. No."

"I see. May I ask if you had an insurance policy on Mr. Parker?"

Evans lowered his head, replying, "It's standard procedure for firms like ours, where we rely on the work of an individual, to carry key man insurance. We would be fools not to do so. We have key man insurance on all our top executives. For instance, we don't know if any of his clients will stay with us. Or even if the new client will remain a client now that Parker is gone."

Dominic asked, "The whale?"

"Exactly, the whale. He'd developed a personal relationship with Parker. Thus, we don't know if he'll remain a client. That's why we carry insurance," responded Evans.

"May I inquire how much the insurance policy was worth?" Dom pushed.

Albert said, "I'm not sure we know the amount at this point. We'd have to review the policy. Do you know?" Albert asked, pointing at Evans.

"No clue," replied Evans. "Let me just say, it's usually a few million dollars. That helps but losing an executive or a partner could cost our firm multiple millions in the long run. You can see that, I'm sure."

"I can, of course," Dom said. "Do you have insurance on each other?"

"Yes," replied Evans. "We have key man insurance that pays the firm in the event of death, just like we had on Jonathan. And, have life insurance to fund a buy-sell agreement between the partners, as well."

"And how does that work?"

Evans replied, "We estimate a value for the business. Suppose, for the sake of argument, they valued the business at…say…ten million dollars. Since we have two senior partners, each owns fifty percent. Therefore, each partner's share is worth five million dollars. In the event of one partner's death, the insurance pays the firm the five million."

Father Dom was listening intently. He was learning something new. "But that's just like the other insurance, the key man insurance."

Albert added, "At first glance, yes. Although, in the buy-sell agreement, we stipulate the funds received from the insurance company be used to buy out the widow or the estate of the deceased partner. Neither of us has any interest in being in business with our deceased partner's wife—nothing personal, of course."

"Parker didn't have this insurance, I take it," asked Dominic.

Evans responded, "Correct, he had not made partner yet."

"I see," said Father Dom.

Albert looked at his watch. "Father, is there anything else? Perhaps, we can continue later. Possibly, you can buy us a drink at your pub. Now, we have a staff meeting scheduled."

"I understand. Thank you so much for your time. You've been extremely gracious," replied Dom, as he stood to shake hands with the partners who were both already standing.

Exiting the conference room, Evans grabbed Dom's upper arm and said softly, "You should also check on a young lady Parker was seeing. I think there was a lot of," he paused, "sinning going on."

Father Dom turned to face Evans. Both partners began laughing. "Do you know who she is?" Dom asked.

Evans replied as he rubbed his nose, "No idea. He called her Marilyn, but we know that's not her name. Parker would say she looked like Marilyn Monroe. We can only imagine."

Albert added, "The S.O.B. would leave us one man short on our racquetball days." The partners laughed again.

Evans added, "I'm not sure, but I think that young lady visited him after his wife's father left."

"You mean before he jumped?"

"I think so. This is a big office. We occupy the entire floor. We don't necessarily know who comes in or when. Guest to the building must sign a register when they come in. Check with them downstairs." Albert replied.

"So, she may have been the last one to see him alive?" Dom asked.

"Possibly, yes," said Evans.

"May I see his office?" Dominic asked.

"By all means. Follow us," said Albert and led the way.

Father Dom inspected the office, which was nicely appointed. Two plants seemed freshly watered. There was a nice leather couch facing a beautiful oak bookcase that accommodated a flat-screen television and a large ornate desk with two finely upholstered chairs in front. A credenza held family pictures in silver frames and awards. In the corner, there was a small conference table with three chairs. Leaning against a wall was a golf bag, bright red with a white NIKE logo on the side.

"Mr. Parker was a golfer, I see."

"We all are. Do you play, Father?" questioned Evans.

"I'm afraid not. Chess is my passion."

"Ah, a thinker," said Evans, smiling and looking at Albert.

Father Dom walked towards the windows. "Which of these was the one Mr. Parker jumped from?"

The partners followed Dominic and again glanced at each other. "This one," replied Albert. He pointed at a window.

"This must have caused some stress in the office."

Evans said, "It has. It was horrible. We've offered counseling to anyone that feels they need it."

"That's appropriate, yes," Dom said. "Was anything in disarray in the office?"

Evans gazed around. "You mean as if there'd been a fight or something?"

"Exactly," Dom replied.

"No," he responded. "Everything was just as it is now."

"Anything else?" Albert asked as he contemplated his gold Rolex watch.

"No. Thank you again, gentlemen," Dom said, walking out of the office and towards the elevators. "Thank you for your time."

As Father Dom walked alone towards the bank of elevators, Kathy came from around a hallway with her head down and waited for the partners to return to the conference room.

Timidly, she said, "Father, I'd like to stop by later. Will you be there after six in the evening?"

"I'll have your Stella ready, Kathy."

CHAPTER FIVE

Mrs. Adelle Parker opened the front door, letting out a puff of cigarette smoke as she greeted me. "Good morning, Mr. Mancuso. Please, come in."

"Please, call me Joey, Mrs. Parker."

Adelle was an attractive lady with short black hair and blue eyes. Maybe forty years old. Impeccably dressed, wearing what looked like an expensive black pearl necklace. I could tell she'd been crying. She picked up a glass with her right hand from a table by the front door and held a cigarette with her left. She pointed to a small office off the foyer's grand entrance.

"Please, have a seat. May I offer you a drink?" she asked.

I glanced at my watch. It was ten-thirty in the morning. "No, thank you, Mrs. Parker."

"Please, call me Adelle. Coffee, perhaps?"

"I'm quite fine, thank you again. You have a beautiful home. This entrance is spectacular. I can see all the way back to the pool and patio area."

"Thank you. What brings you out to North Bergen, New Jersey?"

"Lovely community. In all my years in New York, I've never ventured out here. Have you and your husband lived here long?"

"We bought this home when Jonathan joined Evans and Albert. That was about four years ago," she said as she began crying.

"Perhaps, I can come back at a better time."

"No, it's okay. You said you were a private investigator. Are you representing the insurance company?" she asked, putting down her drink and wiping her eyes with a tissue.

"We like to keep our client's names private. You understand," I replied.

She put out the cigarette in a large thick, expensive crystal ashtray and pulled another from the pack lying on a coffee table. She asked, "Would you like a cigarette?"

"No, thanks. I haven't smoked cigarettes in years. That's a beautiful ashtray, Mrs. Parker. Is it Waterford crystal?"

"It is, yes. It was a gift to Jonathan from a client. He has two more in his office, as well."

"Did Mr. Parker smoke?"

"Nasty habit. Jonathan and I both smoke. We enjoyed a drink and a cigarette together, but now..." her voice trailed off.

"Tell me about the insurance policy, if you don't mind."

"Which one?" she asked, taking a sip from her drink.

I could smell the single malt, "Start with one of them," I said, not knowing how many there were.

"We have two. An old one for half a million and a new one for two million."

"How new is the last one?"

"I've already contacted them. They said they'd review the matter. That's why I thought you're working for them. There's a clause in the policy that if the insured commits suicide before the policy is in force one year, they don't pay," she said, her voice trailing off again.

"I see. And has it been less than a year?"

"That's the thing. He bought the policy, but it took him a month to get a physical and get approved. I don't know when the policy took effect. It's a little after a year now."

"Why did he take out a new policy?"

"I was worried that if something happened to him, it'd have a devastating effect on me."

"Everything seemed to go well for him. Business-wise," I said.

"For him, maybe. But he invested my trust fund with his company. Last month, we received a letter saying that our returns had gone down from twelve percent per year to four percent."

"You were getting twelve percent per year?"

"Ever since we moved the account to them four years ago, yes. Twelve percent per year was the steady return."

"Mrs. Parker, may I ask you how much is in the trust account?"

"Call me, Adelle, please. I think the balance is a little under four million dollars. My father created the trust accounts for my sister and me."

"The trust is for both?"

"No, we each have a trust of the same size."

"Both managed by Jonathan's firm?"

"Yes, unfortunately. It incredibly upset my father at the news."

I did my math quickly and asked, "You were receiving an income of about five hundred thousand a year from the trust?"

"We were getting forty thousand a month, yes. And now, with Jonathan gone, his income lost, and the return on the trust at about a third of what we were getting, I'm afraid I may have to sell the house. It devastated my sister. She has two small children in a private school and no husband. The meager twelve thousand a month won't suffice for her either."

Not for your lifestyle, no. I wanted to say. "What if you closed the account, retrieved the money, and did something else with it?"

"My father asked them to do just that. The thing is, they claimed the money is in non-liquid investments. Alternative investments, offshore certificates of deposits, and real estate. I know nothing about that."

"When did your father ask for the money?"

"He's been asking for a month. As soon as we received the letter. He was there at Jonathan's office yesterday before he jumped. Feels horrible, thinking he may have been the catalyst for Jonathan taking his life.

"He was there before Mr. Parker jumped?"

"Yes, before he jumped. Oh, my God, what am I going to do?" she said as she started crying again and got up from the settee. "Can I get you a drink?"

Right now, I could use one, was what I thought. Instead, I replied, "No, thank you, you go right ahead." I wanted to ask about Ms. Melody, but I didn't have the heart to do so. "Was everything good between you and Mr. Parker?"

"What couple doesn't fight? We loved each other. We were even thinking of adopting a child. We couldn't have one ourselves. He was such a romantic person."

Of course, he was. "Does your father live in New Jersey?"

"Manhattan. East Side. He's retired."

"I assume he's wealthy?"

"He was lucky in life. He sold his company a few years ago for forty million and gave his daughters ten percent each in a trust."

"Where is his money invested?"

"Guess where? He was one of Jonathan's first clients at the new firm when he started there. Jonathan asked him to move everything over when he joined Evans and Albert."

"That's what's called all the eggs in one basket."

"I'm afraid so. Dad didn't want to do it, but he did it for me. I feel terrible now," she said as she lit another cigarette.

"I may want to talk to your dad. Could you arrange that?"

"As soon as he comes back, I'll be happy to do it."

"Where did he go?"

"Some island in the Caribbean where part of the money is invested in certificates of deposits. He's trying to retrieve that part."

Good luck with that. "One last question, Adelle. Is there another reason, besides the issue with the investments, that you think Mr. Parker may have wanted to take his own life?"

"None whatsoever. He was excited about a business trip to Portugal and Spain. He said he had excellent potential new clients to meet there."

"Were you going with him on these trips?"

"He never wanted me to go. And I understand. He said they're boring meetings, lunches, and dinners with small talk all the time."

"I can imagine, yes. I understand that he was about to make partner at the firm?"

"Indeed, he was. The new account he just got is so big, they offered him a partnership."

"He must have been happy about that, right?"

Taking a long drag from her cigarette, she replied, "Yes and no. On the one hand, a partnership is what he strived for. It meant a considerable increase in pay, bonuses, and participation in all profits. Plus, other perks. Something bothered him about accepting it."

"Did he share his concerns with you about that?"

"No, he was very reserved about his work. He always said he never wanted to burden me with his work."

"I see. May I call you if I have other questions?"

"Mr. Mancuso. Joey. Please, feel free."

"Mrs. Parker, thank you so much for your time, and again, I'm sorry for your loss," I said, getting up and heading to the front door.

"Thank you. Good luck with your investigation. Please, call me if you find anything else," Mrs. Parker said as she closed the door.

CHAPTER SIX

My next destination was a visit to Doctor Death. I took an Uber ride back to New York and the coroner's office.

I began writing my notes from my meeting with Mrs. Parker as we continued to Manhattan. She had given me no sign that there was a problem with their marriage. Of course, I didn't expect she would, had there been. So far, I had two conflicting stories between Mrs. Parker and Melody. The mistress knew more about the deceased than the wife.

Arriving at the OCME, or the Office of the Chief Medical Examiner, some old friends greeted me as I headed to where the body of Jonathan Parker was to be examined. After securing my visitor's badge, I walked in to see more old friends.

"Doctor Death, how the hell are you?" I said to the ME in charge.

"Detective Mancuso, what brings you to my dungeon? I thought you'd be in Florida wearing silly plaid Bermuda shorts and driving a golf cart by now," the ME asked.

"Too young for that shit, Frankie. There'll be time for that at some point. Tell me, do you have the body of Jonathan Parker here?"

"We did an autopsy this morning on him. Why would you be asking about that?"

"And your conclusion?" I asked, ignoring Frankie's question.

"He's got a variety of broken bones, severed spine, massive traumas. The COD is consistent with the fall that killed him."

"With all the years you spent in school and the exhaustive experience you've gained here, you say the fall killed him?"

Taken aback, my buddy, the ME, stared at me and asked, "Are you going to challenge my conclusion on this, Mancuso?"

"Doctor D, I don't think the fall killed him," I replied, seriously.

"Then what did?"

"The landing, Doc, the landing," I said, laughing.

"Once an asshole, always an asshole," the ME replied, relaxing a bit.

"Suicide?" I asked.

"Unless you have proof to the contrary, yes."

"No defensive wounds?"

"None apparent, no. Why are you asking?"

"Can I see the body?"

"Again, why are you asking?"

"My brother and I are private investigators now, and there's an insurance issue involved. If it's suicide, the widow is out a few million dollars. If not, the insurance company is."

"And you guys represent whom?"

"We're private investigators, with an emphasis on 'private,' Doc."

"I see. Walk over with me and peek. By the way, are you smoking again?"

Shit, I must really have picked up this smell from Mrs. Adelle. "I stopped that habit many years ago. Call it a 'transferred smell.' How can you even smell that in here? All I smell is the odor of death."

"Those of us working here become accustomed to that smell. The odor of death, as you call it. However, we become very sensitive to outside odors. Such as cigarette smoke."

We walked to where the bodies were stored in refrigerated facilities. Doctor Death opened Parker's niche. Rolling out the body, he said, "What are you hoping to find?"

"I don't know, Doc," I replied, shocked by the injuries to the body. I thought for a minute about what goes through the mind of a person falling to his death. Does your life really flash in front of you?

As we both looked at the broken body, Frankie asked, "Are you thinking he was pushed out the window?"

"Something like that, yes."

"If so, they have surprised him from behind. Because there are no signs of fighting off an attacker. No defensive wounds. Of course, falling twenty-one floors can disguise many things. He's full of contusions, abrasions, and lacerations which are consistent with the fall. Make that the landing."

"Right. Any blunt force trauma?"

"He has a penetrating trauma here," said his buddy. He raised Parker's head and pointed to a section on the back of the head just left of his right ear.

I examined it. There was a triangular penetration. "How big is that?"

He peeked at his notes. "The penetration itself is seven-eighths of an inch high. The indentation is almost a ninety-degree triangle."

"A ninety-degree triangle?"

"That is correct."

"What's the overall size?"

"If it was a rectangle, it'd be almost an inch by half an inch in total size."

"What the hell could make an indentation like that?"

"Nothing comes to mind."

"What do you think? Take a guess."

"It could have been a rock he hit when he landed or any other object that caused that trauma on the landing. Or part of a window he hit on the way down."

"Did you examine the scene?"

"Does a dog lick his balls? Of course, we did, Mancuso."

"The penetration. Could it have been caused by something hitting him on the head before the fall? Is there any way to tell?"

"Not unless you find an object that fits the penetration, no. You think someone hit him and then pushed him?"

"Let me ask you, is it possible?"

"No one suspected any foul play. The autopsy is done because they ruled it a probable suicide at the scene."

"The keyword being 'probable.'"

"I suppose he could have suffered that blunt force trauma prior to the fall."

"So, there is a possibility of foul play?"

The doc thought for a second. "I could say yes to that, yes. But, not enough to change the COD."

"Did you determine the time of death?"

"Not to an exact time, no. He landed on a second-story ledge. From our examination, he must have laid there at least an hour before the body was discovered."

"Had rigor mortis set in?"

"No, that takes at least four hours to set in."

"When are you releasing the body?"

"Services and cremation are scheduled for tomorrow."

"Shit, cremation?"

"That's what I understand, yes."

"Can you hold the body an extra day?"

"Not without catching a lot of shit from everyone. We're late as it is. It's been busy here."

"I'll owe you, Doc."

"Yeah? How are you going to pay me?" Doctor Death said, laughing.

"I own Captain O'Brian's Pub in the Financial District. How about you and your staff come over for happy hour one day? Drinks on me?"

"No well drinks, only premium."

"You've got it, Doc, thank you."

CHAPTER SEVEN

Father Dom was already there when I got back to the pub. He was meticulously writing down and studying his notes from his interview with the partners at Parker's firm. He was anal about his organization. I stood behind the bar, and Dom sat on a stool in front of the bar with his files opened.

The bar, designed by Dom's grandfather, was an incredible piece of work. It ran the length of the establishment on the left side. Beautifully worn solid dark oak wood and mirrors covered the entire wall behind the bar, with glass shelving to hold the liquor bottles and glasses.

"How did it go, Brother?" I asked.

"Interesting. Did you know that the wife, her father, and what's her name were there the day he supposedly jumped?"

"Melody, the big-breasted lady, was there?"

"Melody, yes. I think she may have been the last one to see him alive."

"That doesn't match my information."

"What? That Melody was there?"

"That and his wife's visit. She told me her father went to see him. She never mentioned that she'd been there. And Melody never mentioned she was there, either."

"Did you even have time to ask her that many questions?"

Mr. Pat, listening to this conversation, smiled.

"Who, Mrs. Parker?"

"No, Joey, Melody. You guys seemed kind of cozy in Woody's booth."

"I conduct my interrogations in various ways," I said, winking at Mr. Pat.

"I'm sure you do. Are you going to write your notes so we can compare?"

"It's getting late, and we need to open the bar in a few minutes. I've got them all written. I was a decorated detective first grade, remember?"

Dom made a face. "Mr. Parker's assistant is going to stop in around six this evening. She seemed concerned when I was there."

"Did she recognize you?"

"She's a patron. We call her Stella."

"Oh, that cute thing. She worked for Parker?"

"His personal assistant."

"I bet she's got a lot more information."

Dom asked, "What did the coroner tell you?"

"Doctor Death ruled it a suicide. However, we noticed a blunt force trauma to the head just above the right ear. It's a right-angle penetration, and it would be an inch by half an inch if it were a rectangle. And almost half an inch in penetration."

"Can he tell if that happened before the jump?"

"No, he can't. However, he agrees with me that it could've been before. There's no way to tell for sure."

"A right triangle? That's an odd shape for an object, isn't it?"

"I agree. Did you get to see Parker's office?"

"I did. Nothing jumps at me. Pardon the pun. Did you know he ended up on a landing, not the sidewalk?"

"Frankie, the ME mentioned that. So what?" I said, grabbing a Brooklyn Lager.

"It seems his body laid there dead for a while before anyone noticed he'd jumped or been pushed."

"Who first noticed?" I asked, taking a sip from my locally brewed lager.

"I didn't ask. That's a good question, though."

"I need to train you better if you want to be a first-grade detective."

"Kathy can probably answer that later."

"Who's Kathy?"

"Stella, the assistant."

"Right. She's a cute young lady. What...in her mid-twenties?" I enjoyed toying with Dom by adding trivial stuff. He was just all business.

"That's about right," Dom replied, asking and keeping his eyes focused on the files and his notes, "Any defensive wounds on Parker?"

"None. If he didn't jump, he was surprised from behind or hit with an object. Then pushed."

Dom glanced up from his notes, "Other than the partners, only Mrs. Parker's father could have the strength to push him by surprise. His wife or Melody wouldn't have the strength to just push him out the window."

"Agreed, unless they struck him on the head, he fell forward on the window, then pushed."

Father Dom stood and began putting all his notes inside the file. "Yes, I'd agree. I wonder if they opened the window prior to the jump."

"Parker smoked cigarettes, which is not allowed. More than likely, he'd open a window when he lit up."

"That'd make sense."

I downed the beer and recycled the bottle in a bin under the bar. "Let me review my findings," I said as Father Dom remained standing in front of me.

I continued, "Mrs. Parker was devastated that he died. Also, because her husband's death eliminates his income altogether. Plus, the returns on investments from her trust account of four million dollars dropped from twelve percent for the last four years to about four percent this year going forward."

Father Dom interrupted, "Where's the money invested?"

"That's the deal. It's with the partners. There is more. She had four million. Her sister also had the same-sized account. And...her father had at least thirty-two million with Parker and the partners. They were all getting twelve percent per year since they moved the accounts to the company."

"How the hell do you get a consistent twelve percent return on your investments? Interest rates are at an all-time low. These guys must be geniuses, no?"

"What's been the return of the indices the last three years? Do you know?" I asked as Mr. Pat opened the bar's front door.

"No clue. We need to check that. Those returns aren't workable. I bet Marcy would know that."

"Why, because she's FBI?" I asked.

"No, because she's into that kind of stuff. She's with the Bureau's White-Collar Crime Division. Besides, she's smarter than both of us."

"You're impressed with Special Agent Marcy, aren't you, Father Dom?"

"She's a professional—and bright."

"Right," I said.

"What else is in your notes?" Dom asked.

"Both Mrs. Parker and Melody forgot to tell me they were there the day this guy died."

Father Dom came behind the bar and opened a Coke. "Listen to this. Both Mrs. Parker and her father were heard arguing with Parker that day."

"That's consistent with what Mrs. Parker told me, except that she was there. It upset her father with the returns on the investments, and they were trying to cash out the holdings."

"So, why didn't they?" Dominic questioned.

"She said they heavily invested them in shit that isn't liquid. Including certificates of deposits in a Caribbean bank."

"CDs in a Caribbean bank? Who does that?"

Just then, Marcy walked in the front door with a large bag. "You guys hungry?" she asked.

"What you got there, special agent?" I asked, smiling at her.

"Four pastramis on rye with melted cheese and four orders of curly fries. You in, Mr. Pat?" she asked.

"You bet, Ms. Marcy. I'll just take another pill for my cholesterol," replied Mr. Pat in his Irish brogue.

The scent from the hot pastrami permeated the bar. "How do they make curly fries, anyway? And, why bother?" I asked.

Everyone made a face, a bit puzzled and ignoring my question.

"Besides bringing lunch, I did some research on Evans, Albert, and Associates, also," Marcy said.

"Wonderful," replied Dom, as he sat back on a stool.

"We were just talking about the investment returns that the partners were able to get consistently. Is it workable to get twelve percent returns four years in a row?" I asked.

Marcy took the sandwiches from the bag and placed them on the bar. She replied, "In 2015, the Standard and Poor's index was down slightly. However, in both twenty thirteen and fourteen, they were up double figures. But, let me tell you, these guys, Evans and Albert, have been paying out twelve percent for longer than four years. According to my research, they've been doing that for almost seven years straight. Because of that, their client list has grown tremendously, including some state pension plans and both public and private unions."

I reached for my sandwich and fries. "How do they do that?"

Marcy gave Father Dom and Mr. Pat their sandwiches and fries. "Remember, Mr. Bernard Madoff? I think he had consistent returns on his fund of about eight percent."

"Good ol' Bernie had a Ponzi scheme going on. How about a Pellegrino, Ms. Marcy?" Mr. Pat asked.

"Thank you, that'd be great," Marcy replied. "A Ponzi scheme in which he was able to pay the returns with the new capital invested by other investors."

I added, "So he wasn't getting the returns advertised, but he was using fresh capital to pay the current investors. No one had a clue?"

Marcy took a sip from her Pellegrino. "Insiders of the firm had a clue. Although, the investors did not know. His returns were fabricated, and there was money missing. Money he was using for their personal expenses. Plus, he got away with it for years and years."

Father Dom put his sandwich down. "And now, he is serving what? One hundred and fifty years in prison?"

"Exactly," Marcy replied. "Wow, this pastrami is good, isn't it?"

Patrick mumbled something in the affirmative.

I said, "Let me ask you something, Special Agent. Isn't our Social Security being run like a Ponzi scheme by our government?"

Father Dom reached for another Coke and said, "Here we go again."

Marcy smiled at Dom and replied, "You can say it is. Our government has borrowed the money paid in by Boomers, who are now retiring, for other purposes. As the Boomers retire and Generation X and Millennials pay into the system, their money is going to pay those who retired."

"Brother, I know what I'm talking about," I said, with my mouth full.

"Fine," Dom replied, "Let's get back to our case. Marcy, do you think these guys are doing the same thing?"

"Very possible, Father. Problem is, there are no complaints to follow, and unless a whistleblower comes forward, there is no reason to begin an investigation."

Four people walked into the bar. Mr. Pat said, "I'll take care of them. You guys go on."

"Sit them towards the front," I said.

"On it," Mr. Pat responded.

I asked, "A whistleblower? Don't they get paid if the tip proves to be real?"

Marcy smiled. "Indeed, they get anywhere from ten percent to thirty percent of the funds recovered. That's *if* it's their information that leads to the conviction and recovery."

I turned towards Dominic. "Interesting. Did you hear that, Bro?"

Wiping his hands and ignoring me, Dom added, "We have the assistant of Mr. Parker coming in later. She appeared a bit concerned when I saw her earlier today at the offices of Evans and Albert."

"You think she's ready to blow the whistle?" Marcy asked.

Shaking his head, Dom said, "She acted worried. I don't know if she has something to say about the suicide or anything else. We'll see when she gets here."

Marcy asked, "What time is she coming in?"

"After six, she said she'd stop by," Dom replied.

"I'll try to come back around the same time. Hope you enjoyed your sandwiches," Marcy said as she got up from her stool.

"Let us pay you for these," Dom said.

"She makes big bucks, Brother. She can afford it," I said, smiling and embracing Marcy. "Can we get together later?"

"I got it, Father," Marcy replied. Turning towards me, she said, "Maybe. We'll see if I can make it back. Then, I'll decide what to do with you."

"I have a few ideas. But before you go, I have one last question," I said.

"If it's not about the case, I don't want to hear it," Dom said emphatically.

Marcy smiled at Dom.

"It's about the case. What do you know about offshore certificates of deposits? Like in a Caribbean bank? Are they safe?"

"I'll cite another Ponzi scheme, Allen Stanford, serving one hundred and ten years in federal prison. He owned a securities firm in the U.S. and a bank in the Caribbean. He, too, paid investors an unreasonably high return on the CDs. It's the old saying. If it's too good to be true, it probably is," Marcy replied.

"That means this whole thing with the partners could be a house of cards," I said.

"Possibly, yes," Marcy replied.

"You see, Father, I told you Marcy was smarter than both of us together. I know how to pick 'em or what?"

Marcy replied, "Mancuso, there's another saying. Don't count your chickens before they hatch. And you didn't pick me. I picked you." She turned and began walking out of the bar.

"Love you, Special Agent," I said, smiling, as she turned back and waved with one finger.

CHAPTER EIGHT

It was a little after six in the evening, and the bar was packed. Lots of energy inside this place. I guess it must have been a good day on the stock market. The Wall Streeters were spending money on good prime liquor and cigars. Father Dom was anxious because Stella, make that Kathy, had not shown up. I was anxious, too. This cute young lady could have some information that could break this case. Assistants usually know as much, if not more, than their bosses about what's going on.

Father Dom came to me behind the bar. "Joey, I'm going to have to leave soon."

"Don't leave yet. This lady, Kathy, doesn't really know me, and it's not likely she'll open to me without you here. You know what I mean?"

"I hear you, but I can't stay much longer."

"Give it a few minutes. By the way, you never shared your observations of the partners earlier today. Any thoughts?"

"In fact, I do have some thoughts, and after hearing Marcy's comments on the Ponzi schemes, I've been able to put a few things together."

"Like what?"

"I think these guys were not being truthful with me. I mean, they talked a good game, but their body language was all wrong."

"You an expert on body language now?"

"Not an expert, but there are things you learn if you're paying attention after a while. These guys had some 'tells' that were obvious."

"Give me the short version," I said, hearing the traffic and looking at the front door. Our second shift of patrons was coming in.

"They're going to collect on an insurance policy they had on Parker."

"There's a motive. Go on."

"You mentioned before that Melody had spoken to one partner, right? Because both said they'd never met her."

"Interesting. Melody told me she had spoken to Evans when he called her on the phone and had met her."

"About what?" Dom asked.

"She was about to fall for the old line. Evans told her he knew an off-Broadway producer who was interested in fresh new faces, and possibly he could hook her up with him. Of course, he had another hooking in mind."

"Is that another motive? Did he want Melody for himself?"

I put some clean glasses in their place. "Nah, I don't think so. Although, men have killed for uglier women."

"Both knew of Parker's ongoing affair with Melody. They refer to her as Marilyn. They said that Parker's playing around would leave them one man short when they played racquetball and laughed about it."

I thought for a second. "They had Parker by the balls. Why can't guys keep their affairs to themselves? They need to show their peeps they are masters of the game, I guess."

"I'm glad you answered your own question because I have no clue."

"What else you got?" I asked, wiping the bar.

"Parker had earned a partnership because of his new account. Which means he was going to get a piece of the firm. Maybe, they didn't feel like giving up a piece. And now, they keep his clients for themselves."

"Another motive. But aren't clients likely to move to another firm since Parker isn't there to service their accounts?"

"Keep in mind that Parker acted mostly as an asset gatherer for the firm. He wasn't responsible for managing the investments. Clients must be happy with the incredible returns the partners produced for them. It's not likely they'll abandon Evans and Albert."

I glanced at Mr. Pat, who was serving drinks to the people in the front. "But the returns they've been getting are going down to four percent. Some clients may leave because of that."

"That's another thing."

"What other thing?" I quizzed.

"Why are the returns going down? If they're running a scheme, perhaps, the cash flow isn't coming in as usual, and they have to lower the cash output."

I glanced around the pub for a Wall Streeter amongst the patrons and spotted a fellow who was friendly and a good customer. I called out to him using his preferred drink order, "Oban, can I talk to you for a second?"

Oban wasn't his name; it referred to the Scotch he drank.

"What's up, Joey, Father?" Oban replied.

"My brother and I are talking investments here. Is it feasible for an investment to return twelve percent for the last seven years?" I asked.

"Wow, that would have been fantastic. Last year, the market was down a bit. This year, so far, it's up about four percent. You can't get a steady return like that unless you're using the capital invested to pay out as flow. But not from returns," Oban said.

I exchanged glances with Dom, turned back to Oban, and retorted, "Right? Get what the market gives you."

Oban shook his empty drink glass, rattling the ice cubes. "You could set the payout at twelve percent per year. However, if the market is not keeping up with your cash outflow, you risk paying out your own capital. What investments are you guys in?"

"It's not us," Father Dom replied. "It's a friend, and they're in alternative investments, offshore certificate of deposits, and some other illiquid stuff. Here, let me refill your drink." Dom gave him an extremely generous pour.

"Thanks, Brother. I mean, Father. I would stay away from offshore CDs, man. You never know who's backing that, and there's no government insurance. Unless you trust some banana government, right?" Oban said as he took a sip of his newly refreshed drink.

"Let me ask you something else," I said.

"Ask away, Joey," replied Oban.

"What do hedge funds charge for their services?"

Oban had had a few Obans already, and he was having trouble speaking clearly. He replied, "Ah, a lot, man, a lot. Normally, they charge a fee for managing the funds. Anywhere between one and three percent. But here's the best part. If there's a profit, they get about ten to twenty percent of that. Big bucks, man, big bucks."

"Thank you. Are you driving home?"

"No, we have a designated driver, you know? See that guy there with the virgin Bloody Mary? He lost. He made less commission than the rest of us today. Dumb fuck. He gets to drive."

"Good, good. Thanks," Father Dom said.

"Any time, guys. If you have some bucks to invest, let's talk about it, okay?"

I walked Oban back to his table.

A couple ran in the bar screaming, "Call 9-1-1. There's been an accident at the corner! Hurry!"

Almost everyone reached for their cell phones and began dialing. Dom's face showed consternation. We both clearly had a bad feeling about this. Running out together, we reached the scene of the accident. We could see a person lying on the sidewalk but nothing else. Neither the police nor the emergency responders had arrived yet.

"What happened?" I asked the crowd that had gathered.

"Man, it was a hit-and-run," someone replied.

"Did anyone see anything?" I asked.

"This SUV drove onto the sidewalk and ran this lady over. Then, they sped up and left. Never even stopped," another person added.

As we got closer, Dom said, "Shit, it's Kathy."

CHAPTER NINE

Kathy was unconscious at the scene. What a freaking waste—such a nice young lady. Father Dom appeared devastated. He was sure it was no accident. No one had gotten a plate number or a description of the driver. It had all happened so fast.

"She's not dead, Father," I said, trying to console him.

"Did you see her body? My God, she has tire tracks on her face."

Marcy arrived at the bar for our dinner date and walked over to the scene of the accident. Make that the scene of the crime. "What just happened here?"

I replied, "It's the young lady who worked at Evans and Albert. Kathy is her name."

Marcy asked, "Coincidence?"

After about twenty minutes, we walked back to the bar as the rescue vehicle pulled out. I was walking beside Dom as he prayed. I replied, "We don't think so. She was coming over to talk to Dom. We think she had some information on the Parker jump or something else."

"So, you think this was an attempted murder to prevent her from speaking?" Marcy queried.

"I don't know, but what a coincidence, right?"

Father Dom raised his head and added, "I don't believe in coincidences. This was premeditated. They must have seen her speaking to me at the office."

"What do we do?" I asked.

Marcy thought for a moment. "We have no proof of anything. We have a suicide that could be a murder, and we have a hit-and-run that could be an attempted murder. It's all circumstantial."

"We need to put this shit together. We can't let whoever get away with this, no fucking way," I said, in a bit of a rage.

"I need to get back to the rectory," Dom said.

"I'll drive you, Father," Marcy said.

"This kind of throws a cold bucket of water on our date, doesn't it?" I asked, facing Marcy.

"Let's drive Father back to Brooklyn. We can still have dinner after we drop him off. Unless you want to join us, Father?"

Somewhat aloof, Dom replied, "No, you guys have your dinner. I need to reflect and pray for this young lady. We'll meet up tomorrow and discuss everything."

After letting everyone know at the bar, we were off and got into Marcy's car. Mr. Pat was always at the ready. After all, he had been running the bar long before we took over. The ride to Saint Helen's was quiet. No one was in a mood to talk much. Traffic was its usual craziness going across the Brooklyn Bridge. Arriving at the rectory, we began saying our goodnights to Dom.

"I can't help but think it was my fault this young lady might die," Dom said.

"Dom, don't even go there. You had nothing to do with this. If she dies, it was the perps that did it. They would have done it anyway if they thought she could reveal some information detrimental to them. You can't blame yourself for this," I replied.

Marcy added, "Father, Joey is right. If she knew anything, and they feared she would speak, it was just a matter of time. We'll sort this out."

"I guess you're right," said Dom, "I just feel...if she hadn't been coming to talk to me...," his voice trailed off.

"Brother, say your prayers, and don't blame yourself. Trust me, you had nothing to do with this," I said, getting out of the car and giving him a hug. "She may still recover from this and be able to shed some light on the matter."

"Have a good night, Marcy, and thank you for the ride."

"You take care, Father. We'll put the pieces together tomorrow," she replied.

We drove off, leaving Father Dom to his own thoughts.

"I don't know if we can put the pieces together by tomorrow, do you?"

Marcy replied, "I have more information on the partners I'll share with you. Should we find a place to eat?"

"Sure, how about Vinnie's?"

"Italian again? Don't you tire of Italian food?"

"Fine, what do you want?"

"How about Aroma's just up the street?"

"Don't you tire of Cuban food?"

"Touché, Joey, touché."

"Aroma's is fine. I'll have their meatballs."

"Meatballs with white rice and black beans. They don't have marinara sauce," she said, laughing.

"Whatever."

We drove for a few blocks to her favorite place, naturally, and searched for a table to sit down. The smell of garlic, fried plantains, and Cuban coffee all melted together into the aroma of Cuba or maybe Little Havana in Miami. It was a quaint little place with white tablecloths. Oil and vinegar and a little vase with a white flower adorned the top of each table. They tiled the floors in a Marimba patterned Cuban cement tile in a geometric and floral pattern copied from the Ferrer Palace in Cienfuegos City in Cuba. Aroma's was family operated since '75 by the Garcia's.

"*Señorita Marcela, bienvenida,*" said Camilo, the proprietor. "Sit at any table, please."

"*Saludos, Camilo. ¿Como esta, Marcia?*"

"In the kitchen. She come out and say hello in a moment," Camilo replied.

"*Gracias,*" Marcy said.

We sat down, and I moved things around, the salt and pepper shakers, the oil and vinegar bottles, and the little vase with the flower.

"Why do you always do that?"

"Do what?"

"Everywhere we go, you move everything around. No matter what's on the table, you rearrange."

"Never noticed that. What else did you find out?"

"You're a control freak."

"Why? Because I move things around?"

She ignored my question. "I did some more digging and—" she started to say.

"Wait, wait," I interrupted, "I'm a control freak? What about when you're in bed?"

"What about when I'm in bed?" she asked in a low voice glancing around.

"You always have to be on the right side of the bed. You need to have the pillows in a certain way and—"

Now, it was her time. She interrupted, "And, I always start foreplay with a—" she paused.

"Okay, never mind," I said, lowering my head, a little embarrassed.

"You don't mind me being in control, do you?"

"So, what else did you find?"

She laughed. "Right. The partners seem to have a cash crunch now. They're tapped out on their credit line for the firm. Evans is behind on his mortgage two months, and Albert had his azure two-door Bentley convertible repossessed last week."

"No shit. You'd never know from what Father Dom told me about their offices."

"I think everything there is falling apart. They've made some bets on the markets that have turned upside down on them. They invested in options, and they went against them, big time."

"I don't know what options are, but I'll take your word for it."

Marcia came out of the kitchen and approached our table as she wiped her hands on her apron. "*Marcelita, mi amor, ¿Como estas?*"

"*Bien, gracias ¿Y usted?*"

"Working hard, my love. Who is this statue of a man?" she asked in her accented English, pointing at me.

"*Este es mi amigo, Joey,*" Marcy said, "Stand up and say hello to Marcia," she ordered me.

"*Ay, como se parece a Charlie Bronson, mi actor favorito,*" Marcia said.

I stood up, and Marcia gave me a kiss on the cheek. "It's a pleasure, *Señora*," I replied.

"Yes, yes, *un placer. Cuídela, es como mi hija,*" Marcia said, looking at me.

"*Sí, sí,*" I replied, smiling back, without a clue about what I had agreed to.

Marcia took away our menus. "No menu. I bring food," she said.

There went my meatballs.

"*El quería albóndigas,*" Marcy said to Marcia.

"*¿Albóndigas? No,* no meatballs," Marcia replied.

Marcia went back to the kitchen. I needed a rapid translation of what had transpired. "What just happened here?"

Marcy sat down, laughing and enjoying the moment. "First, no meatballs for you."

"Why?"

"She wants to bring you something else. It will be fine. Then, she said you must take care of me, 'cause I'm like a daughter to her. Also, you resemble her favorite actor, Charles Bronson."

"Tell her Bronson liked meatballs."

Marcy laughed as she took a sip of the sangria Camilo had brought to our table.

I ate some hot Cuban bread with too much butter, which was delicious. "Is *amigo* how you say boyfriend?"

"Hah, no. It's the word for friend. *Novio* is boyfriend."

"I am not your *novio*?"

"I don't know. Are you?"

I began rearranging the breadbasket and the sangria on the table.

"To be continued, I guess," said Marcy. "Back to the story. The Department of Justice, coincidentally, just asked us, our White-Collar Unit at the FBI, to investigate possible insider trading transactions the partners may be involved in."

"This is getting interesting. So, you're getting involved?"

"They did not assign me to this investigation, but I'm in. I told my boss I had some information, and she agreed."

"That's great. What's the plan?"

"I'm going to talk to the partners tomorrow morning."

"Are they expecting you?"

"The FBI doesn't make appointments."

"Oh, my God. What is that on that plate coming over here?" I said as a plate of something fried and twice as big as the plate itself was placed in front of me.

"That's *palomilla empanizada*," Marcy replied, smiling at the server.

"If you say so. It resembles a chicken fried steak," I replied, still trying to figure out how to start on this thing.

"It's a breaded beefsteak."

"A beefsteak?" I cracked but smiling.

"You'll love it," Marcy added.

"So, it's like a cubed beefsteak breaded and panfried."

"Delicious, yes."

"It's the whole damn cow. Breaded!"

"You are so vulgar. Eat it. It's great."

Just as I was planning my attack, the server brought me another plate full of aromatic white rice with tiny little pieces of pork bellies and garlic over the rice and a big ass bowl of black beans that had its own incredible bouquet.

"Did you tell Marcia to kill me or something?" I asked.

"Leave room for the *guayaba y queso*."

"I don't know if I'll be able to have sex after this meal," I said as another plate of fried plantains was placed. "Really? Just who were you planning on having sex with tonight?" Marcy snapped as she prepared to eat her own enormous meal of what she called *arroz con pollo*. It had a delicious, distinct fragrance. I could smell the cumin. Yellow rice and chicken. She had translated for me.

"I thought we would—" I stopped. "No? You didn't have the same idea?"

"Make up your mind, *amigo*. If you want a relationship, it must be monogamous. I don't have time for an open relationship. My clock is ticking, and it's time for me to settle on someone who's serious."

"If you've got some ticking going on, you need to have it checked by a doctor."

"You are such an idiot."

"Who broke up our serious relationship before, *amiga*?"

"I had a reason. It petrified me, you working on the force and not coming home one night."

"You work in law enforcement. What's the difference?"

"I'm working white-collar crimes. They don't shoot at you, usually."

"Tell that to Parker and Kathy," I said, immediately regretting my statement.

"Fine, you made your point. Listen, my dad died in Vietnam, and I can't ever forget my mother's suffering. I've always had that in the back of my mind. And when my brother, Arturo, deployed to Iraq, the waiting and praying began all over again. One whole year, both Mom and I prayed and worried. Fortunately, he came back to us in one piece."

I reached over the mass of food on the table and grabbed Marcy's hand. "I'm sorry. I should've never brought this up. You never shared those fears before."

"I know. I'm sorry, too. We had a grand thing going, and I blew it."

"I didn't stray too far. Now that I'm a business proprietor, things are different."

"What about the issue with monogamy?"

"*No hablo español*," I replied, laughing.

"Are you always going to be an asshole, Mancuso?"

"You turn me on when you say Man-cu-so like that. It's so sexy."

"So?" she asked, raising her fork and knife threateningly.

"What? Am I going to be monogamous or an asshole forever?"

"Both."

"Yes, and maybe."

She smiled a wonderful smile. Opening my mouth, I pointed to my teeth with my index finger.

She asked, "What?"

"You have yellow rice stuck on a tooth."

She closed her mouth, truly concerned that she had something stuck on a tooth. She was so easy.

Marcy drank some sangria and said, "And here I was, going to take control and start foreplay with a—" She paused. Lowering her voice and covering her mouth with both hands, she softly finished her sentence.

"Check please, Camilo," I said, a bit too loud. "Let's head to your place."

CHAPTER TEN

We proceeded to Marcy's apartment. Camilo hadn't given us a bill. Dinner was his and Marcia's treat, he said. I left the server a hefty tip. As much as I'd wanted to make love to Marcy, and she to me, I'm sure we were both bummed out about Kathy's accident. Of course, the enormous meal didn't help either. My plan was to wake her up to a passionate lovemaking breakfast.

Something was bothering me about one partner. Evans, to be specific. Somehow, I knew he was a big political donor, but there was more to his name that kept me up tonight than thinking about him. Around two in the morning, I sat in Marcy's living room alone. After two servings of bicarbonate of soda to relieve my accumulation of gas, it came to me.

My premature departure from the NYPD was due to, according to my captain, my unconventional ways of solving cases. I had a feeling that case was related to Evans, somehow. Unfortunately, all my notes and case files were kept confidential after my retirement. The case had gone unsolved.

They had assigned me the homicide of a homeless person who was murdered in an alley behind Manhattan's celebrated 21 Club. The victim wasn't identified, and they listed him as a John Doe. No prints on file, no DNA, nothing on Mr. Doe. Because of that, the case became a low priority. And me being in the shithouse already, it rolled down to me.

Witnesses said that day, prior to the murder, they had seen two well-dressed men arguing in the alley. The one witness had identified one of the two men as possibly a candidate for the U.S. Congress. In fact, the victim was one witness who saw, or at least claimed to have seen, the same person, the candidate, in the alley with the second man. The COD had been a blow to the head with a blunt object. My initial investigation had ruffled some big feathers because I'd requested from the 21 Club the list of guests who had reserved a table for that evening.

I could not get the list from the restaurant voluntarily. I requested we issue a warrant. That was when the shit hit the proverbial fan. The assistant district attorney assigned to my case told me I had no reason for such a request. She added there was no cause for me to think that it involved the club or any of its patrons in the murder of Mr. Doe. The toxicology report on the victim showed he'd been intoxicated the evening he was murdered. The other witness, also homeless, was never seen again after the initial statements he'd given to the police on the scene.

None of this sat well with me. First, I didn't give a shit the victim was a homeless person. In my book, he was a person before he was homeless, and his murder deserved a resolution. Someone had taken the life of an innocent person. If the higher-ups didn't want this case solved, they should have never assigned this freaking case to me. The captain knew my reputation. I took my assignments seriously, and I was always relentless in pursuing a case. So why me?

Second, all the obstacles thrown my way made me just that more resolute in finding the perp or perps responsible for this senseless killing. Could it, in fact, have been a fight between two homeless men like the captain and the ADA kept telling me? Sure, it could have, but why the roadblocks? And who were those two mysterious men who'd been seen arguing?

It had set me back five hundred dollars the next day to take Marcy on a date to the 21 Club. This place was a New York institution open since the time of Prohibition. It was a place for the rich and famous, neither of which I was. However, I put on my Sunday best and never revealed to Marcy why we were there. She later disclosed that she thought I was going to propose that evening. I felt guilty about not telling her the reason, and that just made me feel even worse.

It startled me when Marcy walked in the living room and said, "It's three in the morning. What are you doing here by yourself?"

I looked up at her. "I couldn't sleep. Too full and too many things on my mind."

"You want to talk about it?"

"Have a seat," I said as I brought the recliner to its seated position.

"Were you sleeping here?" she asked as she sat on a couch next to me and put her feet up. She was sexy, disheveled, wearing long pajama pants and a white tee shirt.

"No, like I said, I've been thinking. Remember when we went to the 21 Club last year?"

"Of course, I do. That night was special. Why?"

"Maybe you won't think so after I tell you why we went there."

"Go on."

"You might recall I was in the third day of a homicide investigation."

"Of a homeless person. I do."

"They had denied me a warrant for the guest list that had reservations the evening of the murder at the restaurant."

"So, you were on a case?"

"Yes and no. It was, also, a special night for me to be there with you."

"But you had an ulterior motive, and you used me as a prop?" she said, a bit angrily.

"Marcy, I would never use you as a prop. That hurts. We had a great time, and I paid full attention to you. So much so that you never knew I spoke to the waiter and the busboy."

"We had a good time. Did the NYPD pick up the tab?"

"I would've been fired if I'd tried to put that in as an expense."

"That makes me feel better."

"Anyway, I could get a confirmation that a candidate for the U.S. Congress was there with Robert Evans."

"Our Evans from Evans and Albert?"

"The same."

"How?"

"Both the server and the busboy identified the candidate and said he was there with a Wall Street guy who frequents the restaurant regularly."

"Do you know how many Wall Street guys frequent 21?"

"I wish I had my notes, but I'm certain that they mentioned his name. He usually reserves table thirty-one, which is also Bill Clinton's favorite table when he's in town. Just thought I'd share that trivia tidbit with you."

"So, what does that have to do with the murder? I mean, the fact those two were there means nothing."

"The server remembers they went out the back and never came back inside. Their spouses were picked up in the restaurant's front, but they never came in."

"And who paid the bill?"

"If you are a regular there, they have your credit card on file. It's classy not to get a bill if you have invited guests."

"You want some coffee? We have to get up soon," she said, laughing.

"I'll help," I said, getting up and heading to the kitchen with her.

"I still don't see a connection between them being out in the alley and the murder."

"I'm getting there. The one witness claimed to have seen the candidate and a second person arguing in the alley. So, we know it was them in the alley."

"What happened to him?"

"Conveniently disappeared."

"Maybe not for him, right?"

"Who knows?"

"You actually think the candidate for Congress and Evans had something to do with the murder?"

"I have no proof. But why ask for my retirement when I was in the middle of a murder case?"

"Maybe because you're a pain in the ass?"

"Take me off the case, but push me out of the force? After sixteen years? No, I was getting close to something no one wanted resolved. That's why."

"How does that fit in with our current case?"

"I don't know yet. Just something to think about. What time are you going to see Evans and Albert tomorrow? Wait, make that today?"

Marcy eyed the kitchen clock, which read four-thirty in the morning. "In about five hours."

I grabbed her hand. "Come on," I said and headed to the bedroom.

CHAPTER ELEVEN
Day 4
Friday

Marcy drove me to the pub early in the morning. Her plan was to walk over to Evans and Albert for her surprise interview of the two men. As I was making some espresso for us, Father Dominic arrived.

"Father Dom, good morning to you," Marcy said.

"Good day to both of you," Dom replied. "Joey, I'll take one of those espressos if you made enough."

"We'll share. Sleep, okay?" I asked.

"I spent the night thinking about Kathy. I called the hospital. She's still in critical condition. She suffered a crushed parietal lobe," Dom said, pointing to the top and back of his head. "There's something still bothering me about the accident," Dominic replied.

"Marcy is headed to the partners in a few minutes. I'll let her tell you why," I said.

Father Dominic heard me, but he wasn't listening. He began, "I can't comprehend how the SUV veered off the street, drove onto the sidewalk, ran Kathy down, and then sped off. It just doesn't fit that it was an accident."

"Let's go with the supposition that it wasn't an accident. Why the hit-and-run?" I asked. "If they wanted her out of the way, why not something less obvious?"

Dom looked at me, "I disagree, detective. A hit-and-run is a perfect cover."

I thought for a second, "Yeah, I suppose you're right."

Marcy said as she stirred some sugar into her espresso, "What if they were watching her? Having seen you and Kathy speak at the office, Father, they realized she was coming to talk to you. That may be the time they acted."

Father Dom thought for a moment. "I can see that. If, in fact, this was a preventive strike, it was extremely violent and sudden. Someone has something big to hide."

Mr. Pat walked in. "Lady and gents, good morning to all." In unison, we greeted Mr. Pat, and he added, "As I was closing the bar last night, someone told me they saw the vehicle that struck the young lady."

We turned to Mr. Pat with anticipation. I asked, "Did they get a plate number?"

"No, all they saw was a black Cadillac Escalade SUV. Deliberately driven onto the sidewalk and struck the lady, they said."

Dom asked, "How about the driver? Did they see who was driving?"

Mr. Pat replied, "No, I asked them that. It was dark, and the SUV had tinted windows."

I took my last sip of espresso and remembered something. "Wait, a second. I saw a black Escalade parked at Mrs. Parker's home when I visited her."

"Was there anyone else there?" Marcy inquired.

"No, as far as I know, it was her and me. So, the SUV parked at their home must be hers or Parker's," I replied.

"Guys, I have to go meet with the partners. I'll see you after," Marcy said.

"Why are you going there?" Dom asked.

Marcy and I looked at each other, and I replied, "She's involved in an investigation of the partners for potential insider information fraud."

"Really?" Father Dom asked. "That may shed some light on this mystery," he said, making a face as he downed his espresso. "Wow, this stuff is bitter."

"It's better with sugar, Father," Marcy said, smiling.

"I'm going with you to the partners," I said.

Marcy retorted, "The hell you are."

"I think we need to go back and talk to all our suspects again. But this time, we'll change it up. Father, you talk to Mrs. Parker and Melody. By the way, check the Escalade for damage. I'll talk to the partners," I said.

"Mancuso, you're *not* going with me to see Evans and Albert. You are *not* part of my investigation. I cannot have you there with me," Marcy added emphatically.

Dominic said, "We still need to talk to Mrs. Parker's father. He's part of our suspect list, isn't he?"

I replied, "Very much so, but he was in the Caribbean. Find out from Mrs. Parker if he's returned. By the way, the body is to be released today to the family for cremation. If so, and if we find the murder weapon, we won't be able to match the head wound to the object."

"Marcy, can you help with that?" Dom asked.

"I can call the coroner and ask that they hold off. But I'm going to get questioned about that. I'm not investigating the suicide," Marcy retorted.

I said, "Tell them you want to make sure the suicide isn't related to your investigation, and you need the body one more day."

"I'll get some shit for that, but what's new, right? You have the coroner's number?" Marcy asked.

Marcy made her call. I expected some blowback from the family. But the guy was dead anyway, so what was the hurry? Unless they were covering something up.

Marcy disconnected her call. "Guess what?"

"What?" I replied.

"They cremated the body this morning. We are S.O.L.," she said.

"Doctor Death promised me he was going to hold off for one day," I said, a bit loudly.

Dom glanced at me. "By Doctor Death, I presume you're referring to the coroner?"

"His name is Frankie," I said, hitting the bar counter with my hand.

Marcy said, "I'm out of here. Let's reconvene here at noon or so."

"I'll call Ms. Melody and Mrs. Parker to tell them I'm coming over," said Father Dom. "What are you going to do, Joey?"

"I'll wait awhile and visit the partners after Marcy is done. Wouldn't want to interfere with an FBI investigation," I said, making a face at Marcy.

She stuck her tongue out at me and walked out. I turned to Mr. Pat. "Mr. Pat, you can't be here eighteen hours a day. Go home. We'll open the bar at two in the afternoon. Come in about four, please."

"Okay, I'll do that. Everything is clean and ready to open. See you then," Mr. Pat said as he walked out. Along with being the manager of the pub, Patrick O'Sullivan was like an uncle to Dom and me. We shared all profits from the pub with Mr. Pat. Just as if he was an owner.

Father Dom and I stayed for a few minutes, comparing notes to make sure we'd advance the investigation by asking the right questions. I was wondering if Ms. Melody would make a move on Dom. After all, she was aggressive. Maybe a nymphomaniac. I'd love to be a fly on the wall for their meeting.

CHAPTER TWELVE

Marcy showed up at Evans, Albert, and Associates wearing her dark blue FBI windbreaker. "Good morning, I need to see Mr. Evans and Mr. Albert, please," she announced, flashing her creds to the receptionist.

"Do you have an appointment?" the receptionist replied, a bit snappy.

"Let them know FBI Special Agent Martinez is here, and I need to speak to them."

"Have a seat. I'll see if they're available."

Fifteen minutes later, Evans' assistant came for Marcy. "Ms. Martinez, follow me, please." They walked to the conference room. "Mr. Evans and Mr. Albert will be right in."

"Thank you."

Another three minutes went by, and Albert showed up alone. "Good morning, I'm Thomas Albert. You must be Ms. Martinez?"

"Yes, good morning. I'm *Special Agent* Martinez with the FBI. Is Mr. Evans not available?" she said with emphasis.

"He may join us in a few minutes. He's tied up in an overseas conference call with a client. How can I help you?" Albert asked in his raspy voice.

"Mr. Albert, I'm with the White-Collar Crime Division of the local FBI office here in New York City."

Albert sat up in his chair. "I see. What can I do for you?"

"This is simply a preliminary discussion. I'm just gathering some facts."

"I'll be happy to answer your questions unless you think I need an attorney present."

"That's always up to you, of course."

"What sparked this visit? Perhaps, you can start with that," he replied, smiling.

"The Department of Justice received an anonymous letter that claimed your firm was involved in the practice of insider trading."

"That sounds like a broad allegation. Do you always follow up on anonymous letters with no facts?" Albert asked, crossing his arms and leaning back.

"I didn't say the letter did not have facts."

"If you had serious facts, this might not be just a preliminary investigation. Now, would it? Sounds more like a disgruntled former employee—or even a client," he said, opening his arms.

"Have you let any employees go lately?"

"I'd have to check, but this is a highly competitive field. Some make it. Others don't."

"I see. How about clients? Have you lost some lately?"

"We always have clients that close their accounts or change firms, for some reason or another."

"Is it possible to get a list of both?"

"We can put that together for you, of course. However, we'll need a warrant. You understand—our clients' files are confidential."

"How many traders and portfolio managers do you have?"

"I assume you're asking about individuals who manage the funds invested for our clients. We have five portfolio managers overseeing different styles of portfolios. Also, we have twelve traders who perform the buying and selling of the actual securities based on the portfolio managers' direction."

"Are you and Evans involved as portfolio managers?"

"Very much so, yes."

"Where do the ideas for buys and sells come from?"

Albert smiled. "We have a network of CEOs that feed us insider information."

Marcy raised her head from her note-taking and peeked at Albert. "Hilariously funny, Mr. Albert."

"We're no different from any other firm. We do our research. Our analysts analyze. We meet, discuss, and then decide on buys and sells."

"From my research, I hear you've been averaging twelve percent returns for the last seven years, and now, you've dropped that return to four percent. Is that correct?"

"You did your research. We've been returning north of ten percent for quite a few years. Last year wasn't a good year, and we've had to drop our return."

"How do you average over ten percent per year for years? The indices certainly haven't averaged that in recent years."

"Now, you're asking about our special sauce. I'm afraid that's not for public consumption."

"Naturally. Let me ask you this. In the last few days, your firm had two employees involved in accidents. Any thoughts on that?"

Marcy saw to her right that Evans had walked into the conference room, but Albert turned towards him and shook his head, no.

"Hi, I'm afraid I'm still tied up," Evans said, stopping at the door. "I'll be in as soon as I can."

"Where were we?" Albert asked.

"One employee dead. The other in critical condition. Both in the last few days."

"We're devastated about that. It's been a hard week for everyone here. Although, why bring that up?"

"Like you said, it's not every day that a company has two employees involved in death or near death in one week, right?"

"Both unfortunate incidents. Parker was an extremely valued associate. He was about to make partner."

Marcy was jotting down notes, "What about his assistant?"

"Yes, Kathy. What a terrible accident. Poor thing," he said, lowering his bald head and eyeing the floor.

"What kind of car do you own?"

"Are you investigating the accident or a complaint about our company?"

"Kathy's accident, as you call it, was a hit-and-run. From witnesses' testimony, it seems it wasn't an accident at all."

"Are you saying someone purposely ran her over?"

"Too soon to tell. Again, do you mind telling me what kind of car you own?"

"I lease a Bentley. However, my lease was up last week, and I turned the car in."

Marcy ignored the lie. As she already knew, the Bentley was repossessed. "Was Mr. Parker involved in the actual management of the assets?" Marcy asked.

"Mr. Parker's role was mostly asset gathering, meeting with clients and new prospective clients. His role in the actual management was minimal, if at all."

"Is it possible that he knew something he shouldn't have known and paid the price?"

"You mean he was murdered? You have an imaginative mind, don't you?"

"Is it possible?"

"It's also possible Parker was involved in something illegal and decided to take his life out of guilt."

"How could he be involved in something illegal? Do you have any ideas?"

"You're the special agent. I do not know."

"I see. May I look at his office?"

He hesitated, thought about it, and finally replied, "Follow me."

With that, Marcy walked behind Albert and entered Parker's office. "Anyone removed anything from here?"

"What has this to do with your letter of possible insider trading? I don't see a connection."

"Mr. Albert, please answer my question."

He sighed, shook his head, and answered, "I don't know. Mrs. Parker was here yesterday and may have taken some personal items."

"His family photos are still here," Marcy said, looking around.

"Like I said, I don't know what she removed."

A tall, hefty man wearing an expensive navy-blue suit entered Parker's office. Walking right up to Marcy, he said, "My name is Stevan Kapzoff. I'm the attorney representing Mr. Albert and Mr. Evans. Ms. Martinez, is that correct?"

"Special Agent Martinez with the FBI, yes," Marcy replied.

"Yes, well, Ms. Martinez, this questioning is over. If you have any further questions, here is my card. You can call me for an appointment," said Kapzoff, as Marcy took his card.

"Fine, thank you for your time," Marcy said, walking out of the office. "I'll see myself out, and I'll be back."

CHAPTER THIRTEEN

Father O'Brian arrived at the North Bergen, New Jersey home of Mr. and Mrs. Parker. They gathered family and friends at the home. Services had been conducted earlier in the morning for the late Mr. Parker. Before he entered, he surveyed the grounds and the cars parked in the driveway and noticed a black Escalade SUV. Walking towards the cars and around the Escalade, he noticed the car didn't seem damaged.

"I'm here to see Mrs. Parker," Dominic said when someone opened the front door.

"Please, come in. I'll get Mrs. Parker," the person said.

Father Dom stood in the foyer as Mrs. Parker arrived. "Mrs. Parker, I'm sorry to trouble you at a time like this."

"Not a problem," she said. "You must be Joey Mancuso's brother."

"I am," he hesitated. "Dominic O'Brian, a pleasure to meet you."

"Have a seat," she said as they walked into the opulently decorated office off the foyer.

A tall bookcase lined one wall. A plush area rug with vibrant colors adorned the dark wood flooring that seemed consistent throughout the home. A unique chandelier hung from the center of the room. The office had a warm feeling to it.

"O'Brian, you said? Half-brother of Mancuso, I presume."

"Indeed. Same mother. Different father."

"One Irish and one Italian. You two look nothing alike. Both your fathers had the stronger genes," she said, smiling.

"I don't want to take a lot of your time. I just want to go over a couple of things with you."

"Go right ahead. What's on your mind?"

"Is your father back from his trip?"

"We expect him back today sometime."

"Was he able to resolve the issues with the Caribbean bank?"

"I haven't spoken to Dad, so I couldn't tell you if he had."

Dom looked around the small office. "Beautiful golf bag. Do you play golf, Mrs. Parker?"

"Oh, that thing," she said, pointing at the red golf bag. "No, that's my husband's."

"Does he have over one red golf bag?"

"No, just the one," she said, glancing away from the bag.

"Did you pick it up from his office?"

"No, the office sent it here."

"Did they send all his personal items?"

"No, just the golf bag, a golf trophy," she said, pointing to it, "and this ashtray."

"Why only those three items?"

"I do not know. Now I have two of the same Waterford ashtrays."

"They are unique with all the cut-glass edges."

"Yes, they are."

"I understand that both you and your father visited your husband at his office the day of...," he paused, "of the unfortunate event."

She thought for a moment. "Yes, we were there," she replied, lowering her gaze to the floor.

"There was an argument between your father and Mr. Parker, I heard."

"My father was outraged at what happened to the investment returns for all of us. I wouldn't call it an argument. More like a discussion."

"But it was a loud discussion."

"My father has a temper, and when Jonathan told him the investments weren't liquid and couldn't be liquidated easily, my father got a bit brash."

"Did they fight?"

"You mean physically?" she asked.

Father Dom nodded.

"Oh, no. Jonathan told him he'd do whatever he could to make sure the return on the investments would increase to the higher levels. He said he would see about liquidating some of the assets without losing money."

"And your father calmed down?"

"There was nothing we could do. We had no recourse. We could not liquidate, so we're stuck. My father understood."

"Yet he went to the Caribbean bank to see if he could get that money back?"

"After Jonathan took his life, he tried that avenue, yes."

"And he left the same day."

"It was a spur-of-the-moment decision. He was anxious about the funds overseas," she said, lighting a cigarette. "Care for one?"

"Thank you, I don't smoke."

"Who are you guys representing?"

"Usually, we don't reveal who our clients are. You understand?"

"Your brother said that."

"Do you have any ideas, and I'm sorry to ask this, but why would your husband take his own life?"

"I've thought about it. It had to be something related to his work. Although, he was about to make partner because of his new two hundred-million-dollar client. He was under a lot of pressure to bring in new assets to the firm because of the recent cut in returns. I mean, he was getting calls from clients on his cell, here at home, and in his office all day long. He was a wreck. He couldn't sleep. He was even avoiding the country club to keep from seeing clients there."

"How about you two personally? Happy?"

"All marriages have hard times, right?" she replied, putting out her cigarette in the ashtray.

"I suppose so."

"We had our fights, but nothing out of the ordinary."

"Again, sorry to ask...but was he faithful?"

"Are you asking if he had a mistress?" She lit another cigarette. Her hands trembling a bit.

"I'm sorry to ask, but...yes."

"He had no time for that. Between work, trips, his golf, and his racquetball games with the partners, we barely had time to ourselves. So, no."

"Mrs. Parker, I don't want to take any more of your time," Father Dom said, getting up from his chair. "I am truly sorry for your loss."

"Thank you," Mrs. Parker said, walking into the foyer.

"One last question," said Dominic, as Mrs. Parker opened the front door. "Did you and your father leave Mr. Parker's office together?"

She thought for a few seconds, taking a drag from her cigarette. "Yes, we did. We took the elevator together."

"And you left Mr. Parker in his office alone?"

"We did, yes."

"Thank you again," Father Dom said as he walked over to a car waiting for him.

"We're headed to the Riverside Apartment complex on the Upper West Side of Manhattan, correct?" the Uber driver asked.
"Yes, thank you."

CHAPTER FOURTEEN

You could hear a tiny drip of water coming from the faucet behind the bar. I enjoyed being in the pub in the mornings. I could see the traffic outside, but it was quiet inside when the place was empty. At certain times during the year, the sun peeked through the stained-glass windows at the entrance to the pub. The rays illuminated the glass wall behind the bar, blasting sun rays throughout the pub. Manhattan is a concrete jungle. Seeing the sunshine come into the bar was a pleasant feature some mornings.

I'd received Marcy's text telling me not to bother going over to Evans and Albert, and I was eager to find out why. I wanted to confront Evans and Albert.

The near-silence was broken by the sound of a car horn from the traffic as Marcy walked into the bar.

"Why did you tell me not to go?" I questioned as she walked in.

"It would've been a waste of time. They called over their attorney while I was there and booted me out."

"I still want to talk to them about the old case. The one about the homeless person who was murdered."

"Joey, you can't work that old case. We have other issues to resolve. Besides, remember, they're holding your file on that closed unless you make an issue of it."

"What the hell are they going to do? Kick me off the force again?"

"They can cook something up. Who knows? Bring charges against you."

"For what? Trying to solve an old murder investigation?"

"You can lose your disability pay."

"What do I care? Someone killed an innocent man, and they're covering something up."

"All in due course. Let's concentrate on one thing at a time, please. Is Mr. Pat here?"

"Not yet. Why?"

"Can I make myself a latte?"

"Be my guest. So, just what did you learn from those assholes?"

She went behind the bar to the espresso machine and asked, "You want to tell me how you really feel about them?"

"Seriously." Shit, it upset me. I wanted to face Evans. I had planned a series of questions for him. But Marcy was right. One case at a time. "Did you learn anything new?"

"I only met with Albert."

"How come?"

"Evans was coming into the conference room, but I noticed Albert motioned for him to stay out. They're hiding something, I'm sure."

"About Parker?"

"That and about their business. His body language was all wrong."

"So, you and my brother Dom are experts at body language?"

"I am FBI, you know, and we learn about these things in training."

"That's why you're a special agent."

"Hey, Mancuso, don't be pissed at me. We're on the same team here, you know?"

She was right. I was pissed and had no reason to take it out on her. "Sorry, Marcelita, *mi amiga*. I'm just frustrated. We have no body to exhume and examine the wound, assuming we find the murder weapon. We have way too many suspects. All have possible motives. And we're conducting an off-the-books investigation with limited resources. Otherwise, everything is peachy."

"I wouldn't say *limited* resources. I have an investigation regarding the partners."

"You think you can parlay that into the suicide case?"

"I have my ways. That's why I'm a special agent," she said, smiling at me as she licked the foam of the latte from her upper lip. "Have you heard from Father Dom?"

"No, he was headed first to Mrs. Parker. After that, he was going to Melody's apartment on the Upper West Side." I said.

Marcy's cell phone rang, and she picked up. I went around the bar and made myself an espresso while she took notes from her conversation.

As she disconnected her phone, she began, "The U.S. Securities and Exchange Commission has received complaints about the partners, as well. They're trying to move in on our case, from what I just heard."

"There's a pissing contest between the two agencies?" I asked.

"Typical stuff. Everyone wants to score points."

"What type of complaints?" It intrigued me.

"By the partners reducing the returns on the investments, they've opened a Pandora's box. It seems many investors are demanding their invested funds back, to no avail."

"That was quite a dramatic change from twelve percent to four percent," I said, watching the foam forming on my espresso.

"It seems the Securities and Exchange Commission has investigated the partners before and found nothing to go on. Now, they're afraid of being called fools."

"I told you. These guys are big political donors. They probably bought their way out of the fire before."

"Yes, but they never put out the fire. Evidently, the smoldering embers remained, and the fire reignited."

"You'd think they'd have a warning bell go off and learn something from it."

"When you have a Ponzi scheme going on, it just grows and grows. You can't end it. If you do, the whole thing comes crashing down." Marcy said.

I replied, "How do people who do that live with themselves? They know it can't last forever, right?"

Marcy replied, "It's like any other crime. They think they can get away with it."

"Like you said before, these schemes just take on a life of their own, and there's no ending to it. I couldn't live with that. Knowing at some point, it may crash in and bury me."

"That's why it's a house of cards," she said.

"Seems to be what's happening here. Except, we have one person dead and another critical in its wake." I said as I drank my espresso and lit a cigar.

Marcy glanced around the bar. "I love the ambiance of this place when there's no one here. It's a cozy place to hang out."

"The cozy feeling is because of the décor. Here you have your typical Irish pub. Nicely worn and comfortable green leather upholstered captain's chairs around the wooden tables in the middle and the dark wood plank floors. The private booths along the left side with the photos," I said, pointing around.

Marcy added, "One of my favorites photos is the one of Dom's dad with George Carlin. I loved Carlin."

I added, "That picture of Carlin and Dom's dad was in 1975. It was the day after Carlin hosted the first-ever *Saturday Night Live* show. Supposedly, Carlin used to hang out here when he was in New York to get away from the crowds. He loved the fact everyone respected his privacy."

"Significant memories, for sure."

Getting back to the case, I asked, "What now?"

"We're getting warrants to pull all the financials on the firm and the partners. Plus, all stock records, buys and sells, customers' statements, etcetera. This time, they're getting a full colonoscopy." Marcy said.

"You think these guys are going to hang around?"

"Why? You think they'll skip town?"

"Shit, I would. I'd just pack it in and fly out of here."

"Where to?" She was curious.

"I'd go to the coast of Montenegro and chill. No extradition treaty."

"Would you take me with you?"

"I'd take you to the end of the world. But you'd have to give up your shield. Would you do that for me?" I asked, turning the tables on her.

"What? And not be a special agent anymore?"

"You'd be my special angel." I knew I was scoring points here.

She didn't respond. "How soon before Mr. Pat comes in?"

I glanced at my watch. "A couple hours."

Marcy came around the bar and put her arms around my waist. "Kiss me, you fool."

CHAPTER FIFTEEN

"I shouldn't be long. Wait for me here," said Father Dom to his Uber driver.

"Sir, we don't get paid for waiting like a cab. Please, call up another car when you're ready. They'll have one here in minutes."

Dom replied, "I understand."

Dom took the elevator to Melody Wright's apartment on the fourteenth floor and knocked on her door.

"Father, please, come in," she said, holding a thick blue towel wrapped around her otherwise naked body.

"Perhaps, I can wait outside," Dom said, rotating his head everywhere around the apartment, avoiding her.

"Don't be silly. Sit here on the sofa. I'll be but a minute. Can I get you anything?"

"No, no, thank you. I'm fine. Take your time. I'm a little early."

"Make yourself at home. Be right back," she said, walking to her bedroom.

Father Dominic saw a nicely decorated apartment. Country French décor, parquet floors with colorful area rugs throughout. The view of Central Park was magnificent.

"Here we go. Thank you for waiting," Melody said, sitting across from Dom. It had taken her less than two minutes to put on a pink one-piece terry coverall that was no better than the bath towel she had been wearing. Her oversized breasts pointed directly at Father Dom. Her hair was still wet and dripped slightly onto her shoulders. "Father, what can I do for you?"

"Yes," he began, again trying to avoid focusing on her breasts. "We're trying to tie up some loose ends. I just have a few more questions."

"Shoot," she said.

"I understand that you may have been the last one to see Mr. Parker before..." he paused, "before the untimely event."

"I don't think so. The last time I saw Jonathan was at the bar. At your bar, the evening before. So, I'm sure someone saw him the next day, right?"

"But I heard you visited him the next morning at his office?"

"Oh, yes. I went to his office, but he wasn't there. I forgot about that."

"Were you told that at the reception desk?"

"No, they told me to go back to his office, but he wasn't there. I waited for a few minutes, and then I left. Why?"

"He wasn't at his office?"

"No, like I said, he wasn't *in* his office. I waited, then left."

"Why did you go?" Dom asked, looking into her eyes.

"After we left your bar, we came here, but he dropped me off. Then he called me from the car and told me the trip was off. He gave me no explanation. And, here I was, all packed and ready to go."

"Go on."

"So, the next morning, I tried calling him, but I couldn't get him on the office phone or his cell phone. So, I went to see him. I wanted to know what happened. Was the trip off? Or was he breaking up with me?"

"Why would you think he was breaking up with you?"

"When we left the bar, he was ecstatically happy, and we normally come back here for...like...a romantic time. You understand?" she asked, pushing her wet hair back.

"Yes, I do. What happened?"

"He got a call from the bi...I mean...his wife. They fought like usual, and then he dropped me off and drove away, didn't even kiss me."

"Right. So, you thought something happened and were worried."

"My goodness, he will not drop me like a hot potato like that. I wanted an explanation. We were supposed to get engaged, after all. I mean, it upset me, Father. Wouldn't you be?" she asked, sitting up and pulling up the top of her pink coverall.

"I suppose I would be, yes. Was the window of his office opened when you walked into his office?"

"Oh, my God, do you think..." her voice trailed off. She covered her mouth. "Had he already jumped? Is that what you think?"

"I don't know. It was right around that time. Did you see anyone else at the office?"

"Just the receptionist, Carla. She is so nice to me."

"No one saw you at his office?"

"No...no one, I guess. Oh wait, they didn't see me, but Evans and another man were walking like out of his office when I was approaching Jonathan's office."

"Could they have been in his office?"

"Yeah, maybe."

"Was anything out of order in Mr. Parker's office?"

"I have to think. I try not to pay attention because he has pictures of her on his desk. It bothers me to see those, you know?"

"Can you think of anything else about his office?"

She thought for a second. "No, Father, I can't."

"No problem. Joey says Mr. Evans called you once about a possible off-Broadway producer?"

She crossed her legs and sat back. "What a sweetheart your brother is. He's not married, is he?"

"Oh, no. I think he's spoken for, though."

"That's different from being hitched. I'm not doing that again."

"That's good, yes."

"Married men have a lot of baggage, you know? All promises, like politicians, all talk and no delivery. They just want you for the moment. Then, poof, back they go to the reason they came to me. No more."

"Life teaches us lessons. Allow me to ask a couple of more things. Tell me about Mr. Evans."

"He called again. Wanted to meet me for dinner and discuss my acting and modeling background, so he can tell his friend, the producer."

"Are you meeting with him soon?"

"We're supposed to talk today. He wanted to have a quiet dinner here in my apartment and take our time going over my *bona fides*."

"He said that?"

"I don't even know what that is. Do you?"

"Your credentials as an actress, I suppose. Are you planning on meeting with him?"

"I have nothing to lose, and I do want to pursue an acting career."

"Have you ever met Mr. Albert, the other senior partner?"

Melody moved uncomfortably in her seat and stared up at the ceiling before answering. "No, I have not."

"Have you ever been to their offices before?"

"Just once. One evening. But Jonathan was the only one there."

"Did Jonathan talk to you about his work?"

"He was stressed out about that. He always said I was his respite from work. Never knew what that meant either, but I guess I made him happy."

"'Respite' means relief from or to take a break from something."

"Oh, now, I know."

"You said he was stressed?"

"They put a lot of pressure on him. Money, money, money, you know? He kept saying that he had to bring in a lot of money and new clients. That's why he was so happy about the new client," she said as tears began forming in her eyes.

Father Dom got up. "Thank you so much for your time. I'm very sorry..." He didn't finish as she embraced him.

"Thank you, Father, for listening," Melody said, not letting go.

Dom pushed back. "Can I ask you another question?"

"Please, go ahead."

"I noticed Waterford ashtrays like that one," he began, pointing at it, "at Mr. Parker's office and at his home. I'm curious about them."

"I gave Jonathan three of them as a gift. He loved them. They are big and beautiful."

"And you kept one here for his use?"

"Oh, no. He never smoked here," she paused and thought for a moment, "I took that one from his office the morning I was there."

"You took it? Why?" Dom asked.

"If he was breaking up with me, I didn't want my gifts there. You know?"

"You said you gave him three ashtrays as a gift?"

"Exactly. He had already taken one to his home, which bothered me. The other two were in his office. One on his desk. The other on the conference table."

"But you only brought one back?"

"That's all I found. This one was on his desk. So, I took it."

"I see."

"Now, the ashtray is something to remember him by," she said, tearing up. "Father, are Catholic priests allowed to date?" Melody asked.

"No, I'm afraid not," Dom replied, blushing.

"Oh, that's too bad," she said.

"Be at peace, Ms. Wright. I'm sorry for your loss," he said, turning and heading quickly to the front door.

Dominic waited to reach the bottom floor before he placed a call to Joey.

"On my way back, Joey. Is Marcy there?"

"Yeah, Bro. See you then," Joey replied rather curtly.

CHAPTER SIXTEEN

I was anxiously waiting for my brother to return to the pub with his reports on the interviews with the ladies. Mrs. Adelle Parker and Melody Wright. Also known as Melody de Amour. Besides a moment of passion, Marcy and I had covered much of what she did at the offices of Evans and Albert. Knowing my anal brother, we'd have to review her findings with him.

"Marcy, I'm going to buy some sandwiches next door. What can I get you?"

"How about a heated ham, turkey, and Swiss cheese on a Kaiser roll?"

"That sounds good. I'll get three. I'm sure Dom would like that."

It was convenient having a deli next door. Many of our patrons would bring in their sandwiches and enjoy an adult beverage and a cigar at our place. We enjoyed not having to deal with food service, so we kept our offerings to liquor and cigars. The owner of Dino's Deli next door couldn't be happier with the synergy we formed between the two establishments.

Entering the bar with the sandwiches, I found Marcy and Dom putting together two four-tops for our use in the back of the bar.

"So, what do you have for us, Brother?" I said, sitting down and passing the food around.

"Thank you," Dom said as I handed him his sandwich.

"What did you get me?"

"A Marcy special. Ham, turkey, and Swiss cheese."

Making a face, my brother, Dom, added, "It's Friday, Joey."

"Yeah, and tomorrow is Saturday. So what?"

"I don't eat meat on Fridays."

Marcy smiled at me. "Father, I thought one pope changed that rule some years ago."

"I continue to abstain from meat on Fridays. It's sacrifice. It gives me great satisfaction to do these things." Dom replied.

"Why? That buys you more brownie points?" I asked. "I know, you're going to get a better seat assignment at the big theater in Heaven."

"Mancuso, you are such a pagan. Father, how about I call and get you their triple cheese melt? It's wonderful," Marcy offered.

"Wow, they call that their *la fusione di tre formaggi* melt. I love it," I added.

"That's fine. Let's get down to work. The first thing I noticed at the Parker residence is that the Escalade sitting in the driveway doesn't have any damage to it. There were a bunch of cars there, but Mrs. Parker confirmed it was her car."

Retrieving the sandwich Dom didn't want, I asked, "Why were there so many people there?"

"They'd just returned from a service held earlier for Mr. Parker."

"Was Mrs. P. grieving?"

"She seemed sad and did shed some tears while I was there."

With a mouthful of turkey, ham, and cheese, I asked, "What else did you find? Is her father back?"

"Why don't you eat and let others who have manners speak?" Dom quipped.

I nodded for my brother, Mr. Manners, to continue.

"No, her father isn't back. Supposedly, he was returning today. I saw the red golf bag there. The one with the white NIKE logo that I saw at Parker's office."

Marcy added, "Today, I noticed the bag *wasn't* at his office. The partners said that Mrs. Parker stopped by to pick up some things."

Father Dom added, "Very interesting. She told me the office *sent* the golf bag to her home. Together, with a large Baccarat crystal golf trophy *and* a Waterford ashtray."

Marcy asked, "Another Waterford?"

Dom added, "He said she has two of the same ashtrays now. One she had at her home. The other came from Parker's office."

I said, "I did see the one when I visited his home."

Dom spoke, "There's a third ashtray at Melody's apartment."

Marcy inquired, "A third?"

"What's up with these ashtrays?"

"They were a gift from Ms. Wright to Parker. Or, so she said," Dom replied.

"But they left other personal items — didn't you say that before?" I asked.

"That's right. Framed pictures of Mrs. and Mr. Parker were still on the credenza and desk. Other stuff that seemed personal was still there," replied Marcy.

I asked, "So, did she go to the office or not?"

Marcy retorted, "Everyone has a different story."

Father Dom became pensive and sat back.

"Go on, Dom," I said, receiving a nasty expression from him.

"Fine, she admitted to having been there with her father that day. She said she left together with her father. Also, she admits to a discussion, albeit heated, but no screaming fight between her father and husband."

I thought for a second and added, "Okay, let's say she lied to me about having been there and seems to be lying about the fight because someone heard a loud one."

Marcy said, "What's a loud discussion to one person could be a loud fight to another."

I bantered, "In Cuban, any discussion is loud, right?"

Marcy snapped back, "You're telling me Italians aren't loud, Mancuso?"

Pointing at Dom, I joked, "Father, when she's mad and calls me Mancuso, doesn't it sound really sexy?"

Father Dom shook his head. "Are you sure you guys aren't married?" He smiled. "One other thing, one partner said she left the office before her father. Meaning her father was alone with Parker. If we believe that side of the story."

"So, what do we have on Mrs. Parker?" Marcy asked, wiping her hands with a napkin.

"Being the trained homicide detective, I'll list the key points," I said, turning to Marcy.

Softly, she retorted, "You are so full of shit."

Dom, having heard that, added, "He is full of himself and that too, Marcy. Go on, Detective."

"So, let me address my fan club here," I said, replying to these insults and motioning as if asking for a group hug. "Numero uno, Adelle Parker had motive and opportunity. Assuming she doesn't know about Parker's mistress, who would add another motive, she was worried about her trust fund and the lack of return thereof. A one-year-old insurance policy for two million dollars, taken out at her request. However, the timing of the suicide, if a suicide, voids that policy because it wasn't fully in force regarding the suicide clause."

Dom asked, "If she will not collect, what's her motive?"

"One of the first things she told me was about the policy. How the insurance company was telling her Mr. Parker delayed the medical exam. And the policy wasn't effective until he passed his physical. She said her understanding was different and thought the policy was already in effect when he died."

Marcy said, "In that case, if it was her, she miscalculated the timing and blew the chance to collect?"

"Indeed," I replied. "What's interesting to note is that she knew the date she thought the policy would be inclusive of a suicide."

Father Dom added, "She may have done herself in. If, in fact, she did it. No husband. No money."

I said, "There is a small half-million-dollar policy in effect, but that wouldn't last her long. Something else, *numero dos,* if she'd waited for Parker to be a partner, he would've had a buy-sell agreement with the other two partners, and she would have collected a portion of the value of the company's worth."

Dom asked, "Did she know about that?"

"I don't think so. She knew about Parker becoming a partner, but I'm sure not about the policy. These two talked little about his work," I replied.

Marcy had waited to ask, "Regarding opportunity, you'd have to think that, assuming she did it, she pushed him out the window somehow with her father watching or helping. Because he was in the office."

"You are absolutely right, Doctor Watson. If she did it, her father is involved," I responded.

Marcy asked, "What's her father's motive? We've established opportunity, but motive?"

"Not having spoken to him," I started, "he's got about thirty-two million dollars tied up with these guys, and he's stuck. His returns are down considerably. So, it is workable that in a moment of rage, he threw his son-in-law out the fu —," I corrected myself, "the window."

Marcy added, "From what we know, he may have been a shrewd business executive. And, if he figured out the partners had a Ponzi scheme going on, he would surmise that his money was totally gone, *adios, nada.*"

Father Dom was listening as his *tre formaggi* melt arrived. Opening the bag, he added, "Now, that would be a powerful motivator. His life's work reduced to a claim in court and no income."

I said, "A claim in court with little chance of recovery if there's no money in the piggy."

Marcy chimed in, "Again, if he did it, then his daughter, Adelle, is involved."

"Not necessarily. If she was out of the room like she said at first, her father could've done it alone," I said, reaching for the other half of the *tre formaggi* melt Dom left sitting on the table.

He blocked my hand with his right arm. "Wow," Dom said.

"Brilliant detective work, right?" I asked.

"No, this sandwich is good. Touch that, and you're a dead man, Mancuso," Dominic said, looking at Marcy and laughing.

"Recapping," Marcy began, "if she did it, her father helped. Although, if she left before, she's now covering for her father by saying she was there with him until they both left together."

"That's why they call it a mystery," I added.

Marcy couldn't help but laugh. "Have you guys done a background check on Adelle and her father?"

"No, that's next," I said.

CHAPTER SEVENTEEN

"Let's talk about Ms. Melody. What's her motive? Did she have an opportunity?" I asked, putting all the garbage from lunch in one bag and throwing it over the bar. "Did she make a move on you, Father?"

Dom began coughing hard. "She actually wanted to know if you were single."

"Did she, now?" Marcy said.

"And what did you say?" I asked.

Dom touched elbows with Marcy and replied, "That you were spoken for and not available."

"About her motive and opportunity," I said, making an awkward escape. "According to what we know, Melody was the last one in Parker's office. She admitted that much."

Dom added, "She admitted that to me when I told her they had seen her there, but she didn't offer that confession when you spoke to her the first time. Also, she said Parker wasn't in his office when she walked in."

"Let's put that aside for a moment. We have only her word for it that Parker wasn't in his office," I said. "Let's find her motivation."

Marcy took over. "That upset her about not going on the trip. Her engagement was off. At least, momentarily. What do they say about a scorned woman?"

I replied, "Hell has no fury like a woman scorned."

"Exactly, remember that." Marcy added, "I think she saw Parker as her ticket to the high life she coveted so much."

Father Dom asked, "That's it? Her only motivation was marrying Parker? Is that enough to kill him?"

"Let's assume," I said, "that Parker told her the affair was off. That it was over between them. She went into a rage, hit him with something, and pushed him out the window."

"We need to find out more about her past," Marcy said. "She may have other motivations. Did she have any money invested with Parker's company?"

"Good question," I replied. "We don't know that."

"Something else on Melody," Dom said. "She has a dinner date with Evans to discuss her acting career this evening."

"What?" Marcy asked, sounding surprised. "In the middle of all this, she's thinking about her acting career?" she asked, standing.

"That's not what Evans is thinking about," I alleged. "Where are they meeting? Maybe we can follow and listen in."

"At her apartment," responded Dom.

Marcy joked, "That's convenient. I'm getting some waters."

Dom inserted, "I asked if she knew Albert, and she replied no to that. Although, her body language told me something different."

"We have nothing that ties them together. But the partners, or at least Evans, did lie about knowing Melody," I said.

Dominic was thinking. I could see his mind working. "Brother, what are you pondering?"

"What if Parker just jumped?" Dom asked.

"Shit, Bro, you're the one that started this whole conspiracy murder theory. Now, you think he just jumped?"

"I'm just saying."

Marcy chimed in, handing everyone a bottle of water, "Wait a second. What about the young girl, Kathy? A car ran her over. And, from the looks of it, it was an intentional hit-and-run."

"Yes," Dom replied. "Possibly, that's related to your theory of the Ponzi scheme. Someone was afraid she knew too much."

"As the trained homicide detective that I am, if Kathy knew too much, that means Parker knew as much or more. You know what I mean?"

"Are you saying," Marcy rejoined, "that the partners are the prime suspects behind Parker's death? Kathy's accident happened before I showed up to speak to them about their alleged scheme."

"Yeah, but they knew they had some shit clogging up their pipes. They have major financial issues, according to you," I said.

Father Dom said, "Let's go over the partner's motivation and opportunity while we are discussing Evans and Albert. Starting with Melody telling me she saw them as they might have walked out of his office before she walked in."

"Sounds timely," Marcy said. "If Melody is telling us the truth and Parker wasn't in his office. Assuming the partners walked out of his office, we can assume they saw Parker last."

"Not so fast," I said. "What if they walked in the office? And like her, they didn't see him there? See, the problem is that we don't know when he hit that landing on the second floor. That screws up our timeline. All five people were there in the office. Assuming the partners went into his office, any of the five could've been the last to see him and shove him out. Right?"

"Okay, so back to the motive by the partners. Let's analyze," Dominic said.

"There's a whole litany of motivators for them," Marcy began. "The alleged Ponzi scheme cover-up. The insurance they're going to collect on Parker's death. The money they need. The ability to keep Parker's clientele and not share a partnership cut for him. I mean, the list is extensive, isn't it?"

Dom asked, "The insurance they'll collect doesn't have the same suicide clause?"

"It may have. Under normal circumstances, his so-called suicide voids the policy in the first twelve months. After that, it's in full effect regardless of the COD," I said.

Marcy added, "Father, that's done to prevent a person from securing a policy knowing they're about to commit suicide and leaving money to the heirs."

Father Dom nodded, "The assumption then is if someone is going to take their life, they will not wait one year to do it."

Marcy smiled. "Exactly. Taking one's life is a drastic move. It's normally associated with a mental imbalance. Someone that depressed isn't likely to wait that long."

I added, "Suicide solves a temporary problem. More than likely, the motivation for the act would resolve itself in some fashion, given time."

"Based on what you both have said," asked Dom, "is it possible that Parker was so depressed with everything crumbling in his life that he took his own life?"

"You're back to this? Really?" I questioned. "He was about to make partner. He was celebrating here the other night. Shit, he even said he was moving to the Big Apple. Why blow all that?"

Dom added with a bit of humor, "We could ask our resident ghost, Jimmy."

I laughed, "That's an idea. All we need is a Ouija board."

Marcy asked, "Jimmy, the resident ghost? Explain, please."

I responded, "Jimmy Hoffa, the union leader, disappeared in 1975, days after visiting our pub with a small group of men. Patrons who saw him here before his disappearance have always said he's buried under the wooden planks behind the bar."

Dom added, "That's a funny story. However, there are reports Hoffa was last seen in his car in Detroit before his disappearance."

"That's hilarious," Marcy chuckled. "Don't want to be a party pooper, Joey. But let's get back to our case. Parker was under a lot of stress. For one, his constant quest for new clients and money," she paused, taking a sip of water. "The current clients complaining about the returns and the inability to cash out the clients because of their illiquid investments. The possibility of him being involved in the Ponzi scheme. That's a lot of stuff going on. Not to mention his expenses keeping Ms. Melody overlooking Central Park."

"So, we close the case. I go back to tending bar. Brother, you go back to Saint Helen's, tending your flock. Marcy, you follow up on the Ponzi scheme."

"Don't be such a hothead, Mancuso." Marcy said, "This murder mystery needs a resolution."

For a minute, I thought this was over. I hate it when people go dead, and no one is blamed. Admittedly, this could go either way. Suicide or murder. My gut was telling me this was a murder—make those two potential murders and five suspects, at least.

CHAPTER EIGHTEEN

Background checks were going well on our suspects. Fortunately, I still had some friends on the force with access to data. Plus, a lady friend, Agnes, who was hot after my brother Dom. Agnes was working at an insurance company. She could research just about anyone and anything. Marcy was taking care of the research on the partners. So, it limited my research through my sources to Mr. Parker and his wife, Adelle Parker. Melody Wright, Parker's hot squeeze. And Adelle's father, Mr. Andrew Huffing.

I opened the bar at two in the afternoon. For a Friday, things were slow with the early shifters, as I called them. While Fridays are busy for happy hour, our clientele of Wall Streeters has a habit of taking off early on Fridays and getting out of Dodge for the weekend. The top one-percenters live in Manhattan. They hang with their kind at upscale local establishments uptown. Others cozy up to Connecticut and their manicured lawns. The rest of the gang goes across the Hudson to Jersey. Our second shifters comprise my unsavory friends, cops, and others. They do frequent the bar, but their shift doesn't start until about six in the evening. Mr. Pat wasn't scheduled to come in until four in the afternoon. That was our custom for the hardworking Mr. Pat on Fridays.

Just before four in the afternoon, Mr. Pat rolled in and joined me in the Andy Warhol booth where I'd stationed myself to do some work on my notes. This semi-private booth had the most worn leather, probably. However, it was the most comfortable in the joint. It was all the way in the back-right corner. In the 1980s, when not at his studio, The Factory, or in the evenings at Studio 54, Warhol would come here to get away from it all. His friends would never think to find him at an Irish pub.

I raised my head when I heard the traffic from the outside. Always my signal that someone had walked into the bar. "Mr. Pat, two assholes wearing cheap suits just walk into a bar," I murmured, leaving it at that.

Mr. Pat asked, "Is this a joke?"

"No," I said. "Two cheap suited assholes just walked into the bar."

Patrick turned his head to see the two assholes make a beeline to our booth.

"Mancuso, we need to talk," said asshole *uno*.

"Detectives Farnsworth and Charles, you guys married yet?" I asked. Detectives Bob Farnsworth and George Charles were NYPD dicks, both of whom I'd had the displeasure of working alongside in my immediate past life at the NYPD.

Mr. Pat, gentleman that he is, said, "Detectives, have a seat here. I was just getting up. What can I get you?"

"It's good to see that someone has manners in this establishment," said Charles. "Two Cokes would be fine, thank you."

I said, "Patrick, make those fountain sodas. Bottles are too expensive for these guys." Charles had been a friend and a nice guy. Until they assigned him to Farnsworth. Then he became asshole *numero dos*. When the situation called for the good cop, bad cop routine, these two couldn't do it. No matter how hard they tried, neither could pull off being the good cop. I said they were assholes, right?

They smiled at Patrick and took a seat across from me. "Mancuso, it's good to see you're still a shithead," said Farnsworth.

"Takes one to know one," I replied. "What can I do for you ladies?"

"Stop the shit, man. We need some information," said Charles.

"What kind of information?" I asked, looking at Charles.

"Are you working the jumper from Monday on Pine Street?" Farnsworth asked.

"Who wants to know?" I asked.

Farnsworth replied, "For a private dick, you're not very perceptive. Who the hell is asking?"

Patrick brought over the two Cokes and set them on the table between us.

I said, "You forgot their umbrellas." Patrick walked away, hiding a smile.

Charles stepped in. "Listen, the mayor called the commissioner. The commissioner called the captain at the precinct. Someone with heavy juice called the mayor, evidently. We were asked to follow up with you. That's all."

"Why me?"

"Joey, we were at the coroner's office," said Charles, using my first name to soften the tone. "We found out from Doctor Death you'd been asking questions about the jumper. So, we figured it was you. We have some questions of our own."

Farnsworth blurted, "Yeah, like who is your client? And why are you investigating a suicide?"

"The first word in private investigator is *private*. Why does everyone seem to ignore that? My client wishes to remain private. Period."

"You want to see how fast you and your priest brother lose your PI licenses?" Farnsworth asked.

I stared at this idiot. I really wanted to reach across the table and pounce on him. "My brother has nothing to do with this."

Charles said, "Evidently, he's been asking questions, too."

"You have files on this?" Farnsworth asked.

"I don't keep files anymore. I memorize everything," I replied.

"Aha," Farnsworth retorted, "they still have a file on you. The captain said to remind you. And we need some answers."

I got out of the booth, and Charles gingerly grabbed my arm. "Joey, just answer some questions, man. We'll get out of your hair. We need to go back with something. You know what I mean?"

I waved over to Mr. Pat. "Please get Detective Farnsworth a plastic glass. He's going out on the street with his Coke."

"Wait a fucking minute," Farnsworth began.

"No, you wait a fucking minute. I don't have to answer any of your fucking questions," I said.

Charles interrupted, "Joey, Joey."

"I'll talk to you. Your partner waits outside, or you go back with nothing," I said.

Charles nodded to Farnsworth, pointing to the front door with his chin. Patrick poured the remaining Coke from the red-faced Farnsworth's glass into a plastic glass with a top and a straw. Farnsworth removed the straw and threw it on the table. He turned and walked out.

"You love doing this shit to him, don't you?" Charles asked, smiling.

"I forgot how much I disliked him," I replied.

He took a sip from his Coke. "I really like your place. Business good?"

"Excellent. I never thought I'd enjoy being the proprietor of a pub."

"You still hooked up with the Cuban bombshell FBI agent?"

"Marcy?"

"Why, is there over one hot Cuban FBI agent? If so, I want to meet her."

"You're married with kids, or did Jenna kick your ass out?"

"Happily married twelve years, brother, who is not bad for being married eighteen, right?" Charles said, laughing.

"Bring Jenna over one night. I'll have Marcy join us."

"I'd like that. Yes, I'll do that. Now listen, brother, what do you know about this jumper that we don't know?"

I didn't want to give out too many clues why we thought this was more than just a suicide. I didn't need the NYPD involved in this case. Especially after finding out there was a call to the mayor. But I wanted to give Charles something to go back with, so he'd leave us alone.

"There's a grieving wife who is losing about two mil in insurance benefits. If this guy committed suicide, she gets zilch. You know what I mean?"

"So, the widow is your client," he said, not as a question but as a statement.

I let him think that and proceeded, "It's a nothing case, just something for us to do. Who knows? We might pull in other clients because of this."

"Do you have any reason to think it wasn't a suicide?"

I said, "We should wrap this up in a few days. They ruled it a suicide. The likelihood that someone had a hand in pushing this guy out the window is a stretch at this point. If anything develops to the contrary, I'll call you."

"Fine, Joey, I'll go with that," Detective Charles said. "Can I pay you for the Cokes?"

"Get the fuck out, man. Be sure to call and bring Jenna. Leave the asshole home."

Charles got up, bumped shoulders with me, shook my hand, and headed out to his sulking partner. My only guess was that the call to the mayor came from either U.S. Representative Stevens, the man running for Congress back then, Evans, or Albert, which added a twist to our investigation.

CHAPTER NINETEEN

Marcy walked in about five-thirty. The regulars knew better than to even glance at her. But it never failed; the newbies couldn't take their eyes off this fiery lady with legs that didn't quit, wearing tight black jeans and a sports jacket, a shield, and a .40 caliber Glock 22 strapped to her thin waist.

"I just got reamed a new one," she said, kind of pissed.

"That's going to be confusing," I replied.

"What do you mean?" she asked, paused, and added, "Never mind. You are so vulgar."

"Have a seat. Relax and tell me about it. How about a Pellegrino?"

"No, have Mr. Pat make me a *mentirita*. I'm off duty, thank God."

I walked over to the bar and asked Patrick for a *Cuba Libre,* which is rum and Coke. In Marcy's case, it was Bacardi Rum and Coke. Cubans in the U.S. use the word *mentirita*, which means little lie. Cuba Libre means a free Cuba. Because Cuba is under communist rule, there are no freedoms in Cuba under the Castros. Thus, the name.

I waited for the drink to be prepared while Marcy cooled off a bit. Walking back to our booth, I said, "Patrick is working on a second one, considering it is two for one until six."

"That's funny."

"Tell me what happened?"

"My boss was all over me. Evidently, they found out I'm helping you with the jumper case."

"I have a feeling I know why, but why do you think?"

"It's a known fact we sleep together, and someone is complaining about you and Father Dom asking about a suicide. So, they put two and two together."

"Why do they call it *sleep together*? I've never understood that. Do you?"

"Joey, this is serious. I'm using FBI resources to help two private investigators on a case that's not even a case. I can get fired for this."

"Okay, we'll just open a bar in the Keys and fuck 'em all."

"Seriously?"

"With your Jimmy Buffett parrot-head tattoo on the back of your neck, your body in a halter top and hot pants tending tables, we'll make a killing."

"If we can't discuss this like adults, I'm leaving."

"Sorry. I had a visit from two detectives earlier in the afternoon about the same thing. Someone called the mayor of New York complaining about Dom and me asking questions about the jumper. So, the mayor called the commissioner, and it came down to these two guys wanting to know why and what."

"Who do you think called? Evans and Albert?"

"Remember, my case with the homeless John Doe?"

"What about it?"

"The two men in the alley that were arguing, they—"

Marcy completed my sentence, "Were the congressional representative and Evans."

"The congressional representative was only a candidate then, but yes, the same two."

"So, you think Evans called the mayor as a push back to our, make that, *your* investigation?"

"It'd seem Evans, or the congressional representative, did, right?" I said as Patrick brought over her second Cuba Libre.

"Thank you, Mr. Pat. They're perfect as usual," Marcy said as Patrick smiled.

A uniformed police officer opened the front door and handed a server a large envelope.

"Ah, my research just got here."

"Who brought it?"

"A uniform just handed it to Alina."

"Thank you, Alina," I said as she handed me the envelope addressed to Don Signori Giuseppe Mancuso. Funny friends I have.

"What's in there?" Marcy asked.

"Everything my researcher at the force can get on three out of the five suspects. Plus, the jumper."

"You're going to get everyone fired."

"Great, we'll hire them for our bar."

A second later, my cell phone rang. I could see who it was from the caller ID. "Agnes, my darling, how you doing?"

"Hi, Joey, is your brother there today?" Agnes asked.

"He should be here about seven this evening for an hour or so."

"Wonderful, I'll stop by and bring my research on your potential perps," Agnes said.

"See you then, darling."

"Who was that?" Marcy asked after I disconnected the call.

"Another potential server if she gets fired, too."

"Why did you call her darling?"

"All my lady friends are darlings, darling."

"What did she want?"

I love it when she gets jealous. "Agnes is like ten years older than me, and anyway, she's hot for Father Dom."

"Get out of here."

"She was my backup for more research on our top five. Just in case my buddy at the force got cold feet. She's bringing over her files, but she wanted to know if Dom was going to be here."

"I'll have to stay for that."

"Father Dom gets really uneasy when she's here. Back to you. What else did they tell you at the Bureau?"

"They want to pull the case from me, but I told them I hadn't helped you in any way. That it was a coincidence that I was working the partners' case, and you were asking questions about one of their employees."

"They bought it?"

"For now. What did the detectives want?"

"They wanted to see our files."

"What did you tell them?"

"I said, I don't have files. I memorize everything."

"Did you tell them why you're concentrating on the jumper?"

"I told them his widow could be out about two mil if he, in fact, committed suicide. And, that we had nothing else."

"They bought it?"

"Like you said, for now."

Patrick was waving the landline phone over his head, motioning for me to come over. I walked over to the bar. Taking the phone from Mr. Pat, I answered, "Hello, this is Mancuso. How can I help you?" The line was dead. I turned to Patrick and asked, "Who was that?"

"He's not on the phone?" Patrick asked with an inquisitive expression.

"The line is dead."

"He said he was Kathy's boyfriend," Patrick replied.

"No shit. What did he say?"

"Kathy passed away a few minutes ago."

"Shit. What else did he say?"

"Not much. He was talking in a hush-hush fashion. He asked for you or Father Dom. When I asked who was calling, he said, 'Kathy's boyfriend.' That's all."

"Did you get his name?"

"He didn't give me a name."

"Shit."

Greeting some patrons, I returned to the booth where Marcy sat.

"Who was that?" Marcy asked.

"The line was dead when I picked up. But the guy told Patrick he was Kathy's boyfriend." I didn't tell Marcy the entire story.

"Huh, I wonder what he wanted?"

"It was about Kathy."

"How is she?"

I looked at Marcy. Immediately, she knew what just happened.

"It will devastate Father Dom," she said, putting her palms to her cheeks. "Did he say anything else?"

"It seems he wanted to but didn't tell Patrick. Unless he calls back, we won't know."

"The receptionist at the partners' office wasn't nice to me, but I can call her. Maybe she'll know who the boyfriend is. I'll call her tomorrow."

"What makes you think she'll tell you?"

"My shield."

"I don't want you doing anything that can get you in trouble with the Bureau. We shouldn't be going over these files while you're here."

"I know how to do it. If she knows, she'll tell me. But, what about the files?"

"I don't know everyone at the bar. I know my regulars, but there are others here who could watch us. Either from the Bureau or from the force."

"Let's go over to my place and review the research."

"Yeah? We can spread everything on the bed and read."

"I think the dining room table would be more appropriate for that."

"Let's wait for Agnes to bring over the rest. Then, we'll take off. Another *mentirita*?" Marcy nodded, and I headed over to Mr. Pat to get her another rum and Coke.

The door to the bar swung open. Father Dom walked in, followed by this exquisite lady wearing a soft clinging summer dress that made her look sensual. She wore big rim glasses with thick lenses. She had beautiful, bright inviting blue eyes behind those. Her long flowing ponytail of thick blonde hair fell all the way to her waist.

"Agnes, how good to see you. Thank you for coming. What can I get you?" I asked as Patrick was preparing Marcy's third *mentirita*.

Father Dom did not know Agnes was right behind him. I think she'd been waiting outside until Dom came in. Dom turned to see Agnes and became uncomfortable immediately.

"Father, say hello to Agnes," I said.

"Hi, Agnes," Dom said, avoiding my eyes for fear I would laugh.

Agnes smiled at Dom. "Father, your homily this morning at Mass was wonderful. It gave me a lot to think about."

"Happy to hear that," Dom said as he walked behind the bar. I think it was his way to put a barrier between him and Agnes.

"Agnes, something to drink?" I asked again.

"Thank you, Joey. I'll have a Pepsi," Agnes replied.

This gave Mr. Pat and me the opening for our *SNL* routine.

"Mr. Pat," I called out, "a Pepsi."

Patrick replied, "No Pepsi. Coke."

I asked out loud, "No Pepsi?"

To which the regulars replied in unison, "No Pepsi. Coke."

Agnes was embarrassed by the routine. Father Dom just shook his head.

"Agnes, have a seat over there with that young lady," I said, pointing to Marcy. "I'll bring your drink right over." I walked behind the bar next to Dom and said in a hushed voice, "She was in church this morning?"

He looked at Agnes to make sure she was far enough not to hear his response. He turned to me and replied, "She's there every morning at six-thirty for my Mass. I think she's stalking me, Joey."

I turned to face the mirrored wall in case Agnes was facing us. I had to laugh at that one. "Have you ever heard her confession?"

Dom shook his head. "I couldn't tell you if I had."

"Yeah, but has she ever confessed about having impure thoughts about you and her?" Of course, he didn't answer that. His expression of disgust was enough to tell me what he was thinking.

"Joey," he whispered. "I find her attractive," he said, almost apologizing.

"So, do I. She's attractive. That's normal. You're a man first. Imagine when she takes off those glasses and lets her hair down. No need to apologize."

"I wasn't apologizing."

"Sure as hell sounded like that. Just go with the flow, Bro."

"No flow. Why is she here?" Dominic asked, changing the subject.

"She did research on all five of our suspects."

"Are we going to review that now?"

"I'm afraid not. Marcy and I are going to take it with us. I'll tell you why later."

"You're leaving?" Dom asked, sounding a bit anguished.

"You'll have to entertain Agnes for a bit. After all, she did all this work for us."

"*Beata Dei misericordia*," Father Dom replied in Latin.

"Brother, there's something else I have to tell you."

"Yeah, about what?"

"Kathy didn't make it, Dom," I said, holding both his shoulders.

Immediately, he made the sign of the cross and said a brief prayer with his eyes closed. "Frankly, I prepared myself for that. I visited the hospital yesterday, and the prognosis wasn't good at all. She was never conscious after the accident."

"Did you meet the boyfriend?"

"No, only Evans was there."

"Evans? What the hell was he doing there?"

"I don't know. He said he and his partner had been visiting regularly."

"We'll factor that into our investigation. Right now, I'm taking off. Are you going to be all right?"

"Yes, yes, go. When did you get the call about Kathy?"

"A few minutes ago."

"We'll talk later or tomorrow."

I made my way over to Marcy and Agnes and excused myself. It delighted Agnes when I told her Father Dom would visit with her for a few minutes. Marcy and I walked out of the bar to the usual glances from the patrons, and I handed Marcy her rum and Coke in a plastic cup.

"I can't drink and drive," she said.

"I'll drive. You drink."

CHAPTER TWENTY

Marcy's apartment in Brooklyn was a reprieve for me. I really enjoyed her place not only because she was there, of course. But also because it was a peaceful abode. I think she had decorated in a *Feng Shui* style. There were flowing soft colors, a trickling water fountain—whatever that style called for, I think she had it. My place? It was a man cave all over. Not peaceful. More like modern-stressful style. I enjoyed Marcy's place a lot more than mine.

"Make yourself comfortable," she said as we walked in.

"How comfortable?"

She smiled, "Keep your pants on. We need to work."

"How about my shirt?"

"Whatever."

I kept my shirt on, just in case. "Who should we target first?"

"Let's start with the most likely suspect. Who has the biggest motivation?"

"The partners?"

"Start with Evans."

We sat around the dining room table. Marcy took notes while I read. "Let's see," I said as I opened the file on my left. The file from my researcher at the force was on the right. "Robert Evans. Born in 1958 in Albany, New York. Married to Elena Muir in 1988. Three children—"

Marcy interjected, "We know all that from our preliminary research, don't we?"

"You're so impatient. I didn't know his wife's name—"

She interrupted, "Please move down the research."

"Fine." I glanced down at the page. "Graduated from Columbia University with a master's in finance and joined Salomon Brothers right out of school as a trainee. Blah, blah, blah. There are a series of complaints filed against him. All of which his company settled with the clients."

"What type of complaints?"

"Some having to do with CMOs, collateralized mortgage obligations, whatever that is, and a couple for unsolicited trades."

"Go on."

"Yes, boss. Left Salomon to join Spencer and Davis as a senior bond trader in New York. The U.S. Securities and Exchange Commission shut down the company after they became insolvent following the bond market debacle in 2008. There are a few months of nothing. Until 2009, when he formed Evans, Albert, and Associates, a hedge fund, until the present."

"Does it show a list of clients anywhere?"

"A partial list. Some endowment funds, pension fund of New Jersey, some private unions, and...ah...a Horatio Stevens."

"The U.S. Representative from New York?"

"Has to be, right? Too much coincidence if it's not."

"What else?"

"Hang on. I'm reading something here. It seems Stevens was one of the original investors in the company along with two of my *paisans*, Vittorio Agostino and Luigi Bellascone."

"There you go," Marcy stated.

"What? Just because they're Italian, they're criminals?"

Marcy laughed, "No, silly. Bellascone has been under federal scrutiny for quite some time. The organized crime division of the FBI has been looking at him. Money laundering and other hobbies associated with criminals. Don't take it personally, Mancuso."

"I won't. What about Agostino? Ring a bell?"

"No, no bells ringing on that name. However, he has the connection to Bellascone. What about finances on Evans?"

"In a second. Elena, his wife, filed for divorce last year. No resolution yet. She's moved out, back to Albany."

"What about finances?"

"*Aspettare giovane, aspettare.*"

"Thank you for the *young lady*, but I don't want to wait to hear about the finances. That's a key element."

"You'll want to hear about his two mistresses."

"Two? At the same time?"

"No, one at a time. He's not a superhero."

"More like a super asshole."

"From 2009, there was Maria Christina from Queens. And, Katerina Rostova, a model and Russian, obviously."

"Still active with Katerina?"

"It would appear so, yes."

"Where does she live? She asked, looking over at the file.

"Upper West Side. Riverside South Apartments."

"Wait...that's where Melody lives."

"Is that interesting or what?"

"Who did this research for you? Agnes?"

"This part, yes."

"Did she research Katerina?"

"She did according to what she wrote here, but it says she found nothing on Katerina. Agnes added a note saying it seems as if this lady didn't exist prior to this."

"Illegal immigrant?" Marcy asked.

"Possibly a mail-order bride from Russia."

"More like a mail-order mistress," she wisecracked.

"Let's analyze the finances," I said to change topics. "Top one-percenters, but currently collateralized up the wazoo. He pledged everything he owns to loans; second mortgage, credit lines, credit cards, private loans, and his stock portfolios have been getting margin calls. This brother is broke. Living on borrowed time, I'd say. Shit, all these guys are candidates for suicide, if you ask me."

"Okay, so we know the pressure is on. Business going down the tubes. Wife is asking for divorce and alimony. Mistress is in distress. Which leads us to Parker's insurance payment to the partners. A temporary stay of execution. Wouldn't you say?"

"Definitely a motive there. Whatever the amount, it doesn't feel like it'd cover their problems. I think they're much bigger." I said, shaking my head.

"I know. That's why I said temporary. These guys are short-term thinkers putting out fires one at a time."

"You need to turn up your investigation of the Ponzi scheme. Because, if there is one, then the new client, Parker's client, is putting two hundred million dollars into their coffers. That solves a lot of problems if they commingle that money with their own account."

"Speaking of that, like I said before, the pushback is strong. Last time the SEC investigated, they gave them a clean bill of health."

"Perhaps the SEC should hire another group of investigators."

"You want to move on to Albert's file?"

"Not really. I'm tired. We have all day tomorrow. It's Saturday."

"What do you want to do?"

"Take my pants off for a start."

"And then what, lover?" Marcy said in a soft, sensual tone.

"Eat something. I'm starving," I said, getting up from the table and heading to the fridge.

Marcy got up and went to the bedroom. She mumbled something in Spanish I didn't want to translate. I was standing in front of the fridge, which is one of my favorite pastimes, when I felt this incredible warm embrace from behind me. My mind immediately registered nakedness, as my middle back was the recipient.

I had to turn, but I had just put in my mouth a large piece of blue cheese that has a distinct smell. Swallowing fast, I turned and embraced Marcy. I avoided kissing her. Instead, I put my chin on top of her head. I pushed down the last vestige of blue cheese. She began unbuttoning my shirt and kissing my chest with her incredibly sensuous lips.

I picked Marcy up and sat her on the granite counter, avoiding kissing her on the mouth. I began kissing her in a slow and meticulous descent, starting with her neck.

She whacked me on the head. She said, "*Idiota,* take me to the bedroom."

CHAPTER TWENTY-ONE
Day 5
Saturday

Breakfast was served next to me. Two eggs over easy, bacon, hash browns, a plain bagel toasted with cream cheese, and *café con leche*. Everything I could wish for in a partner, I had in Marcy. She was kind, loving, considerate, a hell of a lover, sweet, spunky, funny, and bilingual. What else was there? Right? Plus, she wore a gun to work. Somehow, I had to convince her to get over some fear she hadn't fully shared and to tie the knot with me this year.

"Good morning, sleepyhead," Marcy said as I cleared my eyes and tried to focus.

"Good morning," I replied between yawns.

"Are you still tired?"

"You're not?"

"I am, but there's work to do before your brother comes over."

"Father Dom is coming over?"

"Unless you have another brother I haven't met."

"Let me help you with the housecleaning. I'll do the cleaning if you do the rest."

"Deal. Then, shower and shave."

"No shaving. It's Saturday."

"Hurry up. Your brother is coming," she repeated.

I finished my wonderful breakfast and hurried with the cleaning chores. Then I jumped in the shower. A few minutes later, I came into the bedroom wearing a tee shirt and boxer shorts.

I made the bed and straightened the apartment. No signs of lovemaking were obvious. Candles were lit. Marcy was delighted. It was as if she was expecting the crew from *Better Homes and Gardens* to come in for an inspection.

"I think your brother would prefer if you wore pants," she said, glancing at my hairy legs as I walked into the living room.

"Right. Wouldn't want him to think we're sleeping together or anything," I said, walking back to the bedroom to locate some pants. I heard a knock on the door as I slipped on some jeans.

"Welcome, Father; how is your morning?" Marcy said, opening the front door.

"Good morning to you both," Dominic replied.

I walked out into the living room again and gave my brother a hug, as was our custom. "I've been thinking about this. Was Agnes at Mass this morning?"

Marcy added, "Oh, I've heard she goes every morning to six-thirty Mass."

"Weekdays at six-thirty in the morning, yes. Weekends, I say Mass at eight and nine. I know you'll ask. Yes, she's there every single day."

I had to know, "Does she stay for the double feature on weekends?"

Father Dom smiled. "No, she goes to the nine o'clock Mass on the weekends."

"How about a *café con leche,* Father?" Marcy asked.

"Sounds great. Did you guys go over all the files last night?"

"No, only one. We got interrupted by this guy who came up."

Dom said, "I don't understand."

Marcy screamed from the kitchen, "Joey!"

"We wanted to wait for you to go over the rest. We know you love this part of the investigation," I explained.

"Guys, sit down," Marcy said, setting down Dom's *café con leche* and an espresso for me on the dining room table.

I brought Dom up to date on the Evans' file. He was appropriately curious about the investors that had helped fund the company. Particularly my *paisans.* Marcy covered the information she had on *Signore* Bellascone.

We moved on to the Albert file. Thomas Albert III. Almost identical to Evans, both started at Salomon, etcetera. Albert had graduated from Harvard with a master's in international finance. They both worked at Spencer and Davis after life at Salomon until they opened the doors to their own hedge fund. Unlike Evans, Albert had no known mistresses and seemed to be happily married to Lillian Stanley, a socialite from Connecticut whose family were also one-percenter. Old money from the lumber industry.

Other than the connection to Agostino, Bellascone, and congressional representative Stevens, who were the three original investors in the hedge fund, there wasn't anything that jumped at us from Albert's file.

Dom asked, "What about the Albert finances?"

"Good question," I replied. "He's tapped out, too, just like Evans. Mortgaged up to his neck, for lack of a better word. He told you his lease was up on his Bentley. Not true. It was repossessed. Their only hope for survival, meaning the partners, is the insurance money on Parker. And if they can commingle the new infusion of cash from the client, the whale's two hundred million, they're set for a long time."

"Marcy, what are you doing on your end with these two?" Dominic asked.

"I'm on Evans and Albert like white on rice, Father," replied Marcy, smiling.

"You've been hanging around Joey too long, Marcy," Dom said.

A bit embarrassed, Marcy added, "Also, I've opened a file on Mrs. Parker's father, Andrew Huffing."

"How come?" Dom asked.

"Just had a gut feeling about the sale of his business a couple of years ago," Marcy began. "It turns out he sold his business, a chain of sporting goods stores, to a Mexican company. And, wouldn't you know it, that company has ties to a Mexican drug cartel in Los Angeles?"

"That's why she's a special agent," I said, rubbing her hair.

Father Dom smiled. "You're talking about money laundering?"

"Precisely," Marcy said, giving me a dirty look and fixing her hair with her left hand. "Forty million dollars for five stores seems a bit exaggerated. The revenue from the five stores, even adding inventory, would have been good for maybe a twenty million dollar sales price. Not forty million."

"This just keeps getting better and better, doesn't it?" Father Dom asked. "Anything in Huffing's past?"

Marcy went on. "Nothing special. Graduated with a business degree from Florida State. Worked for a manufacturer of athletic socks. Joined Sports Authority as a top executive. He opened his stores, Andrew's Sporting Goods, in 2010 until he sold them two years ago. Divorced with two adult daughters."

"You're still investigating?" Dom asked.

"My unit is, yes. We're researching the sale of his stores and the cartel connection."

"I want to get to Melody. As you've been speaking, I've read her file, and wow. I hope she has a hundred-thousand-mile warranty, 'cause this young lady has been around the block a few times," I said.

Father Dom removed his white collar and opened the top button of his black shirt. "What do you have?" he asked.

I was smiling as I began discussing Melody, "Born Susan Ashen in San Diego in 1986. That makes her thirty years old. She's worth about four million dollars, as we speak."

"Four million?" Dom asked, clearly shocked.

Marcy added, "That's a lot of modeling."

I went on, "No record of schooling. Although, I think she graduated from Grifter U with magna cum laude. As Susan Ashen, she was the mistress at twenty-two of a movie producer in Hollywood, California. Unnamed in this file. Later, at twenty-seven, she changed her name to Suzanne McIntyre. Married to a William Molden. Divorced a year later. She picked up over two million in a settlement from this dude. She drifted east to New York, and guess what?" I asked, raising my head and opening my eyes wide in anticipation of a guess from my two admiring fans.

Not seeing anyone take a guess, I said, "Ready?"

"Please, just go on...without the drama," Dom said.

"You guys are no fun. Mrs. McIntyre became Susan Osmond and hooked up with Vittorio Agostino. Who, bad boy that he is, is currently married and has been for thirty years to one wife?"

"Agostino was one of the original investors with Bellascone and the New York congressional representative Stevens in Evans and Albert, correct?" Dom asked, again rhetorically, I think.

"*Sí, padre,*" I replied. "The same."

Father Dominic and Marcy both sat there, flabbergasted. Dom finally said, "So, our Melody becomes a mistress to Agostino. Then, to Parker? My goodness."

"It looks that way, yes. Or, she is with both," I replied.

Marcy asked, "Could Melody be a plant by Agostino and the partners to keep tabs on Parker?"

I responded, "That's a possibility. The partners are concerned that Jonathan Parker may have known too much about their operations. So, they hook up Melody with Parker."

Marcy sat back, "And we have a mystery Russian mistress with Evans in the same building?"

I added, "Remember when President Kennedy was rumored to have Marilyn Monroe as a mistress. She was allegedly the mistress of a Mafia boss?"

"No, Joey, you're wrong about that. It was Judith Exner who was Kennedy's mistress while she was Sam Giancana's mistress at the same time." Marcy corrected Joey.

"How do you know so much about that?" Joey inquired.

Marcy explained to him she had been interested in the Kennedy story for years. She told him that Miss Exner was involved with another mob boss named John Roselli.

"Well, I think Marilyn Monroe was a part of the trio," Joey said.

Marcy exclaimed, "Yes, yes. She was supposedly involved with Robert Kennedy and Sinatra, too. Seems our Melody not only looks like Marilyn, but she is following in her footsteps."

Dom said, "Let's review this a second. We have Evans with the Russian mistress. Then, we have Agostino tied to Melody when she went by a different name. Then Melody becomes Parker's mistress. Is that correct?"

I turned to Dom, "That's what it looks like. Amazingly, all in the same building."

Dom added, "We may need to hire Agnes. Her research is incredible."

"We can't afford Agnes unless we get some paying clients. Besides, she makes too much money, and she loves working *pro bono* for us. But you're going to have to cut her some slack. Maybe, invite her back to the rectory and share some wine with her sometime."

"If I may change the subject," frowning, Dom began, "Marcy, is the FBI eyeing Agostino?"

"The FBI's Organized Crime Task Force has been looking at Bellascone. No reports of any investigation on Agostino. At least, not that I'm aware of," replied Marcy.

I went on. "So, the question is, how is our Melody tied to Parker, and did someone plant her there?"

"How does this all tie into Parker's and Kathy's death?" Marcy asked.

Dom got up from the table and walked around. "Marcy, you have a beautiful place here."

"Thank you, Father," Marcy replied, poking me on the arm.

"Just beautiful," Dom repeated. Walking back to the table, he asked, "What about Kathy's boyfriend? Anything new on that?"

Marcy replied, "I'm calling the receptionist on Monday. She was snippy with me. I'll call her."

"Let me do that," Dom said. "She was nice to me. Carla, I think her name is."

I probed, "Why wait until Monday? Call the office now. The way things are going, they're probably working around the clock to contact the clients that dealt with Parker."

"Hand me the phone and the number," Dom replied.

We had our work cut out for us. There were so many things to follow up on. We needed arms like octopuses to deal with everything on our plates. Finally, Father Dom hung up with Carla.

I asked, "What did she say?"

"She whispered, but I got a number for Kathy's boyfriend."

"Call him," I said.

"Did he call for you or me at the bar?" Dom asked.

"I remember Patrick saying he asked for both. Call him."

"I feel horrible. He's still mourning," Dominic said.

"I can call him, but who better than a priest at a time like this?"

"I suppose you're right. Okay, I'll call him."

Marcy was in the kitchen preparing some tuna sandwiches for all of us. I asked, "Marcy, is anyone working this case during the weekend at your place?"

"I'm sure we have some people on it. Why?" she replied.

"We need to wrap this up soon. The longer it takes, the more watered down it could get."

"There's a lot to do. Murders sometimes take years to solve," Marcy added.

"Not for Mancuso, they don't," I replied.

"What are you going to do?" she asked.

"I have some leads I want to follow up on. Then, I need to head over to the bar and help Mr. Pat open. You?"

"I'll head to the office and work on this, too. No sense staying here."

"Are you stopping by the bar later?"

"I'll call you. Sleep here tonight. Tomorrow is Sunday."

"Sleep?"

Mischievously, she said, "You know what I mean."

Dom came into the kitchen. "Arturo, Kathy's boyfriend, is going to meet me at the bar later. Poor guy, he's taking it hard."

"You have an Uber waiting?" I asked Dom.

"Calling one now."

"Excellent. We'll share one back to the city," I said. "Later, *amiga.*"

"What about your tuna sandwiches?"

"Thank you for those. Here, we'll eat them on the ride back," I said.

"Bye, father," Marcy said.

"Be well," he replied. Turning to me, he asked, "What's our next move?"

"Let's talk in the car."

CHAPTER TWENTY-TWO

We sat in the back of this Chevy Caprice. We ate our tuna sandwiches and spoke little.

Finally, Father Dom broke the silence. "Where to now?"

"I'm following up a lead on my last case with the force."

"The one that got you kicked off the force?"

"The same. The homeless John Doe that was murdered," I said, noticing the driver eyeing me via the front rearview mirror.

"You miss being on the force, don't you?"

"To be honest, I do. What I don't miss is all the red tape, all the crap, and hoops you have to jump through these days."

"Are you satisfied with what you're doing?"

"Man, I love working with you, and I love you," I said as again the driver looked at me. I said to the driver, "Father Dominic, here is my brother, blood brother, *capisce paisan*?"

The driver replied, "*Non ho detto nulla, signore.*"

"No, but I know what you were thinking. Just mind the road."

"Yes, sir," he replied, turning his gaze forward.

"What did he say?" Dom asked in a hushed voice.

"That he said nothing."

"How did you know he spoke Italian?"

I touched my hair and whispered, "The grease."

"You're so full of shit."

I smiled at Dom. "Listen, I really enjoy working the bar. I never thought I would, but I do. And spending timing with you is—" I paused "—is a blessing. Besides, now that I don't wear a gun and hopefully no one is shooting at us, maybe Marcy will come around, and you can perform the ceremony at your church."

"That's wonderful news. Has she agreed?"

"I'm working on it. There's still something holding her back. Once I know what it is, I'll overcome it. She's everything I want, Dom."

"Let me know if I can help."

"We'll have to conspire on that. I like it."

"Back to your old case; what's up with that?"

"My former partner, Lucy, remember her?"

"Yes, I do."

"I spoke to her, and she thinks she's located the other homeless guy that disappeared after the incident."

"Really, where?"

"Somewhere in Jersey. One of her CIs has a lead on this guy, the other homeless guy."

"This was the guy that saw—" he started.

I interrupted and opened my eyes, nodding forward with my chin.

"Got it. This is the guy who may have seen these other two characters in the alley behind the 21 Club?"

"Correct," I replied.

"Well, well, that could be interesting."

"Right? Imagine if we can put all these pieces together and solve not one, not two, but three homicides. We'll get a civilian commendation from the mayor. Well, not from the mayor, if he's involved," I said as we both laughed.

"I'm loving it," Dom said.

"You ever wish you'd joined the police force?" I asked.

Father Dom put his head back and closed his eyes for a second. "I wanted to. But our mother prayed so hard for me to go into the priesthood. With my grandfather having served in World War Two and Dad in 'Nam, she felt so lucky that both came back alive. She didn't want the anguish of me being close to guns of any kind."

"Did you have a calling, actually? I mean, does He really call?"

"I feel blessed for the work I do and have no regrets. Did I have a calling?" he asked, not expecting an answer. He continued, "When you spend your childhood in Catholic schools, the brothers and the sisters, but especially the brothers, they're in constant recruiting mode. They tell you that, in fact, He is calling you every day. You just must open your heart and listen, they say. So, between Mom's prayers, her fears, and the Man calling, I guess I heard something and answered."

"You think Mom had an ulterior motive?"

"What d'you mean?"

"Come on. Mom was fifteen when she got married to your dad. You think you were a backseat event somewhere in Brooklyn? And Mom, like me, saw you as our ticket to the Pearly Gates?"

He gazed at me with a horrified look on his face. Our mother was sacred to both of us. She'd been very young when Dominic was born and became an adult too rapidly. An Irish mother as she was, family and her two boys were of paramount importance in her life. We were fortunate she was still with us, albeit in Florida.

"Relax, relax. I was just kidding."

"The problem is, I've always suspected that, and I've prayed every day that God forgives her, if so."

"Listen, she'll be going to heaven and meet with your dad, the Master Sergeant, and my dad, the Mafiosi. Maybe not my dad. He wasn't related to you, so he doesn't benefit from having a family member as part of the church."

"Meaning?"

"I've always heard that if a member of your family is a priest, nun, or brother, you're in. No questions asked. It's like the new express lane at the airport. You're pre-approved and ready to board."

"So, you think that's how it works?"

"Do you know any different?"

"I can't say that I do, no."

"There you go."

Father Dom glanced out the window. I could tell his mind was back on the case. "What are you thinking?"

"Joey, we didn't discuss the background on Adelle Parker or her husband, Jonathan. Anything I need to know?"

"Not much there. Married just the once to Mr. Parker. A middle-class upbringing until the sale of her dad's business. The only money she has or had are the funds her father gave her when he sold the sporting goods business. Active in some charity foundations. A nondescript past and present."

"Was that an outright gift her father gave the sisters?"

"No, they, the sisters, were listed as ten percent owners of the stores. Otherwise, Mr. Huffing would have had a huge gift tax to contend with."

"Still, we think her motivation could be the funds she's losing?"

"That and the potential she knew about Melody and the supposed divorce. If that were to happen and she lost her money, she'd be out cold. Except for a settlement upon the divorce, of course."

"From what you said about Melody, she may not have been with Mr. Parker to get married to him, right?"

"Who knows what her motivation or role was in this mess? Maybe Melody truly fell in love, or maybe she was acting the entire time and was a plant."

"All those various names she's had, did she legally change any of them?"

"No, she didn't. She just took on unique identities."

"What about Jonathan Parker?"

"Our victim. Nothing much negative on him. Graduated from the University of Michigan with a degree in finance. Attended Wharton Business School. Worked for another Wall Street firm for a few years before joining Evans and Albert four years ago. No customer complaints. No black marks on his record. I think this guy was straight. Other than getting hooked up with our Melody," I said.

"I'm no psychiatrist, but I really don't see this guy jumping to his death, do you?" Dom inquired.

I thought for a second. "We've seen him at the bar a few times. Didn't seem any different from our other Wall Streeters. Yeah, stressed out over his business and the stock market. But then, these guys and gals all appear the same. High energy, outgoing personalities, expensive suits and watches."

"Plus, he was celebrating the evening before his demise," added Dominic.

I pondered that. "Perhaps he saw his entire world crumbling in front of his eyes. Upset clients. Losing some of them. Letting his wife down and her father with the money they entrusted in him. Who knows? Possibly even losing Melody over this. Not to mention knowing, or finding out, about the alleged Ponzi scheme, maybe. Something happened that morning in the office that triggered the jump or the push."

"What a beehive this whole thing is," Dom said.

"More like a hornet's nest, if you ask me."

CHAPTER TWENTY-THREE

Dom was going to wait for Kathy's boyfriend, who we hoped had some added information that could make sense of this whole thing. I was going to meet up with my old partner, Mrs. Lucy Roberts, and follow up on the lead we had about the homeless guy.

Lucy was quite the gal. She was but a couple of years away from full retirement. African American, Lucy had been married since she was young to former Army Master Sergeant Harold Roberts. They had three grown and well-educated children. If you opened the dictionary under 'perfect family,' I'm sure there'd be a picture of the Roberts family.

I think she learned the toughness she'd displayed at work from the sergeant. After all, those guys didn't take any shit. Neither did Lucy. Or maybe Mr. Roberts learned his toughness from his wife. Much of what I learned as a detective, I learned from her. She was relentless in her pursuit of the truth. She never gave up on a victim's cause. I was inspired by her and always thought of her as my second mom.

I saw a plain wrapper park illegally in front of the pub. Unmarked police cars are sometimes called plain wrappers. The whole idea is not to look like a police car. Yet, somehow, everyone could tell they were cops' cars a mile away.

Lucy walked into the bar with her usual radiant smile. "Joey, my favorite Italian."

"How good to see you, Ms. Lucy. I bet you say to all the Italians," I replied, hugging her.

"Just you, honey, just you."

"Something to drink before we take off?"

"I wish, but I'm good. We can't hang here too long. I don't want to miss this guy at the homeless shelter."

"You sure you want to go? I mean, I can do this alone. After all, I ran into a problem because of this case."

"This was our case, baby, and we're going to see it through together. Besides, this guy is waiting to see me. Don't know if he'll open up to you alone."

"Let's do this," I replied, walking out with Lucy.

Riding with Lucy in the plain wrapper reminded me of our time together working homicide for the NYPD. She always wanted to drive, and I would not argue with her about that. Lucy reminded me of Oprah in one of her heavy phases. Except Lucy was close to five feet ten inches tall, just one inch shorter than me. If she wore heels, forget about it. I was excited to meet this fellow. Maybe, just maybe, he could shed some light on his buddy's murder that day behind the 21 Club. And now that my new jumper case included Mr. Evans as one of the potential perps, that made it just that much more interesting.

"Lucy, does anyone else know you and I are riding out to meet this fellow?" I asked as she pulled out.

"I have told no one. No, why?"

"Cagney and Lacey are behind us in a dark brown plain wrapper."

She laughed and said, "You mean Farnsworth and Charles?"

"The same two, yes," I replied.

"I try to stay away from those two. Are they tailing you or me?"

"Must be me they're tagging along with."

"What's up with that?" she asked, raising her eyes and peeking at them in her rearview mirror.

"I'm working on a private case, and they stopped by asking questions about it. It's really a coincidence, but this fellow, Evans, is involved in my new case."

"You're kidding? He's the one that applied the pressure to get you thrown out last time, isn't he?"

"I think the same. And I think he's doing it all over again," I said as Lucy entered the Holland Tunnel on our way to Jersey.

"That should tell us something. Joey, are you still dating that skinny-ass Cuban FBI agent? Marcy?"

I laughed. Marcy's ass wasn't skinny by any means, but I wasn't arguing with Lucy. "Still dating her, yes."

"Tell you what. Harry is making his world-famous short ribs Sunday for lunch, and I'm making that rice Marcy taught me how to make. The one with the black beans and rice mixed. What was it she called it? Moors?"

"That would be *moros*."

"*Moros*, right. Anyway, come over about two in the afternoon. I'm sure Harry would love to see you guys again."

"Your kids in town?"

"Just two of them. They're off for the summer. Why?"

"Want to make sure we bring enough Cuban bread and *flan* for dessert."

"Oh, wait 'til I tell Harry. He's always asking about you."

"We'll be there. Why don't you try to lose Cagney and Lacey?"

"Give me a minute. Those assholes will not know if they're in Jersey or Brooklyn in a few minutes," Lucy replied, making some turns into alleyways and side streets. Even I was getting dizzy.

Forty minutes later, we arrived at our destination. *Sans* Cagney and Lacey. There were the usual gatherings of homeless folk in the front milling around. Some going in and others walking out.

I asked, "How are we going to know who it is?"

"I got that covered, baby. He's inside, and I'm supposed to ask for the director of the shelter who is going to take us to him."

As we walked inside, we received the usual looks when plain-clothed police visit a shelter. Somehow, they all think we're coming for one of them. The place was clean with painted cement floors, rows of tables, and posters with positive affirmations on the walls. The air conditioner was blasting cold air, which was a pleasant relief from the summer heat in the streets.

The shelter director took us to the back, where a handful of men were doing dishes and helping with the cleanup after their lunch.

"Ed," he called to one man, "this is Mrs. Roberts. Remember, we spoke about her. Don't worry about what you're doing. We'll take care of it."

Ed turned to greet Lucy. "Hi, Mrs. Roberts, the name is Edmonton Daniels. Please, call me Ed," he said with a friendly smile as he dried his hands on a blue dishtowel.

Edmonton was about ninety pounds if that. Five feet, six inches, at the most. Probably, he was in his late sixties but seemed at least seventy-five. Short cropped white hair, well shaven, and cleanly dressed. Lucy introduced me as a friend. Ed nodded, inspected me up and down, and evidently approved of me being there. "Follow me to my place," he said.

Lucy touched my arm, and we followed Ed. "Ed, you don't live here?" I asked.

"We save the rooms upstairs for those that need them the most. The elderly and sick. I can still manage. I come here to use the showers and to help with the meals."

I thought that was very honorable and took a liking to Ed at once.

"I have something to give you in my place," Ed said as he looked around.

CHAPTER TWENTY-FOUR

Kathy's boyfriend Arturo was late, and Dom feared the worst. He kept himself busy around the bar, organizing glasses, lining up the liquor bottles, and wiping the bar counter clean over and over.

Finally, a fellow of about twenty-five walked in. Clean-cut, wearing a light blue suit and a black tie. He was thin but fit. His features revealed that his parents were of mixed race.

"Father Dominic?" Arturo asked, seeing Dom behind the bar.

"Yes, Arturo, good to see you. I am so sorry about Kathy," Dom began.

Arturo lowered his head and shut his eyes to prevent the tears from flowing.

"Let's have a seat at this table," Dom said, walking to the middle of the pub where our tables are and pointing to a table.

Father Dom pulled out a chair with its back to the front door, but Arturo moved around and chose a chair facing the front door. Something had this fellow spooked, and obviously, he wanted to monitor who entered our pub. Dom wanted to make some small talk, to break the ice somewhat, to make Arturo feel more comfortable.

Dom asked, "Can I get you anything?"

"No, I'm fine, Father. I have little time. I need to get back to work. But thank you."

This was a good opening for Dom. "Where do you work?"

"I'm with Evans and Albert," he said in a low voice. Again, repressing his tears.

"What do you do there?"

"I'm an analyst training to be a portfolio manager."

Surprised, Father Dom rubbed his hands and asked, "What's your role as an analyst?"

"I do research on the securities before we add them to the portfolio I'm assigned to."

"I didn't know there was over one portfolio."

"Yes, the hedge fund manages three different funds. A growth portfolio called Alpha. A fixed income portfolio called Gamma. The one I work on is a balanced portfolio called Stable."

"Can you share anything about the funds?"

Ignoring the question and speaking in a low voice, Arturo said, "Father, I've done some things I shouldn't have."

"Can you elaborate?"

Arturo pulled out an envelope from his jacket's interior pocket. Glancing around, he asked, "Are we alone?"

"We are. Tell me, how long had you and Kathy been together?" Dom asked, eyeing the envelope.

"We've been dating for two years," Arturo replied, composing himself. "I want to confess something, Father."

This took Dom by surprise. "I'm not ready to hear confessions at the moment."

Arturo interjected, "No, not Father."

Relaxing a bit, Dom replied, "Okay, go ahead."

Arturo went on for a few minutes telling Dom about his relationship with Kathy and disclosed a few interesting things relevant to the partners and the manner they managed the various funds. He then revealed some of the papers that were inside the envelope he'd brought with him.

The conversation ended abruptly when Mr. Pat walked into the pub.

"Who is that?" Arturo asked somewhat nervously.

"It's fine. That's our manager," Dom responded.

Mr. Pat waved as Dom nodded to him.

"That's all I have, Father. I must get back to work now. Can you keep these papers safe?"

"Not to worry. We'll do everything we can to solve this and bring to justice those that are involved."

"I trust you will, Father."

"May I ask you one last question?"

"Yes, of course."

"Did you call the police with any of this information?"

He lowered his head again and said, "I'm afraid not, Father. I don't trust too many people. I only talk to you because Kathy liked you, and you're a priest."

"Okay, Arturo. May God be with you."

"And with you, Father," Arturo replied and walked out of the pub.

Dom sat at the table. He went over the documents that lay open and took out his notebook, jotting down a few things. He smiled.

***

Marcy was back at her office, FBI headquarters, at 26 Federal Plaza in New York City.

Victoria, Marcy's boss, approached her, "We upset the SEC that the FBI started a new investigation after they already completed their own investigation. And, in a few words, they told us there was no case to pursue regarding the insider trading allegations."

Marcy replied, "I expected, at least, the DA's office to follow up on the new tip received about insider trading. Hoping that since these two agencies compete for convictions, the DA would at least continue their own inquiry."

Victoria got closer to Marcy. In a hushed voice, she said, "Yes, but the response was a resounding no."

Marcy argued, "There's a potential money laundering scheme going on, but we have no proof at the present time. At least, they should let us pursue that."

"Like you said, we have no proof," Victoria said, "and I'm not about to risk my job on that. In plain English, they told us to cease and desist any further probing into Evans and Albert."

"How can we get proof if we can't investigate?"

Victoria ignored Marcy's comment and added, "You're reminded you cannot aid your boyfriend, former NYPD detective Joey Mancuso, with what some are calling a personal vendetta on his part against Mr. Evans."

"Mr. Mancuso is exploring the suicide angle on his own. I have nothing to do with that," retorted Marcy.

Victoria was losing her patience. "Mancuso is concocting a homicide out of a clear suicide case, and he's trying to implicate Evans."

Marcy thought for a minute and remained silent.

"Marcy," Victoria began in a calmer tone, "if you assist him, you might face a disciplinary hearing with a minimum penalty of being reassigned to some forsaken field office somewhere in the world. Is that what you want?"

Marcy was fuming as she sat back in her cubicle. "Understood."

Victoria walked away and turned back to Marcy. "Collect all your files on this case and turn them over to me within the hour. I'll assign you a recent case involving some Russian bond certificates that were suspected of being forgeries."

"That case has been around forever."

"That's right, and they have not solved it. Your turn to take a crack at it," Victoria said emphatically.

Frustrated, Marcy called Joey on her cell phone. Joey's phone went into voice mail, and this pissed her off even more. She left a message, "Joey, I have a fresh case. Some bullshit about Russian forged bond certificates. This case has been around for years. And now, they want to pursue it again. The case of Evans and Albert is closed on our end. I'm pissed. I hope you guys come up with something. Later."

Part Two
CHAPTER TWENTY-FIVE

Edmonton gave us a valuable piece of evidence he'd cautiously saved for some time. Gingerly, Lucy bagged the item and placed tape around the ends. She placed the item in the trunk of her car. Upon her return to her precinct, she'd enter the item into evidence. We had no clue if it would lead to something, but a clue is a clue. I noticed I had a voice mail from Marcy, and after listening to her message, I texted her to meet us at the pub later.

I turned to Lucy and said, "I want to make a stop before we get back. Do you have the time?"

"Where do you want to go?"

"It'll only take a few minutes. I want to check something out."

"Point the way, Detective Mancuso," she replied, amused.

The ride back to Manhattan's Financial District through the Holland Tunnel was smooth. Lucy and I reminisced about some of our old cases, and I could explain what our current case was about and how it could tie Evans to both instances.

Arriving back at the pub, I saw two familiar faces sitting in their car about half a block from our front door. I waved at Farnsworth and Charles. That garnered a one-finger salute from the driver's side of the plain wrapper.

After saying goodbye to Lucy and promising we'd be at her home Sunday, I walked into the pub to see the smiling, red-bearded face of Mr. Pat. He was getting ready to open at two in the afternoon, and Dominic was sitting at a table with an exuberant look on his face.

"Is Marcy here yet?"

"Not yet," Mr. Pat replied.

Father Dom was smiling. "Mr. Pat," he said, "get Joey a Macallan 18 neat and the Rocky Patel cigar he likes. Joey, come on back, little brother, and have a seat."

"Macallan 18? You fox, what have you got?" I said, pulling out a chair and sitting down.

Patrick brought over the single malt and my cigar, and Dom told me about the conversation with Arturo. He showed me the documents Arturo had handed him.

I was feeling good and went over our conversation with Edmonton. The item he'd handed us was on its way to the evidence locker at the precinct.

Taking a slow sip of my single malt, I said, "It's been a pleasant afternoon. This is great."

"The information we got?" Dom asked haughtily.

"No, the Macallan 18. Good choice."

"I have more good news," Dom said, with a snide expression.

"More? Let's have it."

"My favorite parishioner called."

"Agnes?"

"Your hunch paid off. She's got additional information for us. It should be in our emails in a few minutes. I asked that she send it to both of us."

"I love it. Except now she's going to email you all the time."

"Shoot, I didn't think of that," Dom replied with a scowl.

Marcy walked in with a moping face. She said her hellos to Patrick, ordered a drink, and sat at our table. "I can see you guys seem to enjoy something. Glad somebody is happy."

"What did you order?"

"A Pellegrino," she replied.

I asked her, "Are you still on duty?"

"Effin, no. Sorry, Father."

Dom smiled and called out to Mr. Pat. "Mr. Pat, bring Miss Marcy a Zacapa Rum on the rocks with two ice cubes, please."

"Wow, we must be celebrating. I'm glad because I need something to cheer me up."

"Sit back and relax," I said, taking a drag from my cigar.

We opened the email from Agnes and were excited to see the results of her new research. We discussed with Marcy everything that Father Dom and I had uncovered during the day.

We had to plan our presentation to the various players, and I, as usual, came up with a brilliant idea.

"Here's what we're going to do," I said, adding, "We'll invite the participants to our reveal on Monday at ten in the morning to gather here at Captain O'Brian's. At which point, we'll play our new and exciting show of whodunit."

"Why not Sunday?" Dom asked.

"Two reasons," I began. "Tomorrow, Marcy and I have a lunch invitation that we cannot miss. It's going to be hard to get all these people to come in on a Sunday."

"Where are we having lunch?" Marcy asked.

"The Robertses have asked us to join them for Harry's world-famous short ribs, and Lucy is making your recipe of *Moros*," I answered.

"What do we bring?"

"The Cuban bread and a *flan*. Harry's favorite dessert."

"Father, do you want to join us?" Marcy asked dutifully.

"My dear, Sunday is a busy day at the church. Love to join you, but no can do," Dom replied.

I added, "Plus, Agnes would be devastated if she didn't see Father Dom tomorrow."

"Father, you should take her out to lunch," Marcy added, smiling.

"Oh, she'll stay for our potluck luncheon tomorrow after the last Mass, trust me," *el padre* said, not excitedly.

"How will you get everyone to attend on Monday?" Marcy asked.

"They will. We're going to make some persuasive calls to them between now and then. Trust me, they'll be here," I replied, smiling and taking a long drag on my cigar.

Marcy raised her Zacapa, Dom his Coke, and I, my Macallan. "To the reveal," I said.

Marcy and Dom, in unison, said, "To the reveal," as we all touched glasses and drank.

My cell phone vibrated on the table. The caller ID read, 'Roberts.' Picking up the phone, I answered, "Lucy, we'll be there tomorrow."

"Joey, it's Harry," he said hurriedly.

"Hey, big guy, we're—" I said, but he interrupted.

"Joey, Lucy has been in a car accident," Harry said.

"Is she all right?"

"I don't know. I'm on my way there now. Are you at the pub?"

"Yes."

"Then, you're only a few minutes from her. I'm further away."

"Where is she?"

"She's on FDR Drive, just before the Williamsburg Bridge entrance."

"I'm on my way. You spoke to her?"

"She won't let the paramedics take her to the hospital until you get there. Something about securing the evidence is what she said."

I got up from the table, but my thoughts immediately went to a planned hit in order to remove the evidence we'd gathered. "Did she tell you what happened?"

"A black SUV hit her from the side. Her car is inoperable, but she won't leave the scene until you get there, man. They wouldn't let her speak much more."

"Harry, I'm on my way. I should be there in a few minutes," I replied, trying to think how best to get there and secure the evidence.

I needed to get to her, but her concern was understandable. If someone hit her to abscond with the evidence we retrieved from Edmonton, they'd be waiting for the ambulance to drive away. If I secured the item, the chain of official custody would be broken, which would make it inadmissible.

'Shit,' I thought.

Then it hit me. I walked outside and located Farnsworth and Charles still sitting in their car. Waving to them to come over was fruitless. They ignored me, thinking I was making fun of them.

I ran to their car, opened the back door, and said, "Detective Lucy Roberts has been in an accident a few blocks from here. Get on FDR, hit the lights and siren, and let's go to her."

At first, they didn't react. Farnsworth was trying to figure out what I just said as he sat there behind the wheel.

Detective Charles shouted, "Farns, let's go, man. Get on FDR."

We headed to FDR Drive with sirens blaring and clearing out the cars in front.

"What's going on, Joey?" Charles asked me.

"Listen to me. Lucy and I retrieved a piece of evidence earlier today. She was going to take it to the evidence locker. It's sitting in the trunk of her car. When we get there, we need to follow procedure and make sure we don't screw this up. I need that evidence."

Farnsworth asked, "What is this about?"

"It's about a case we worked together that went unsolved. She got a tip yesterday about a witness," I replied, not wanting to be too specific.

"Is that where you guys were headed this morning?"

"Exactly." At that moment, I realized that if this was an intentional hit on Lucy to remove the evidence, our witness, Edmonton, was in danger. Someone knew where we'd been and surely must know about our witness. "Give me the radio," I said.

Charles glanced back at me. "The radio? What do you want with that?"

"Just give it to me, please."

Farnsworth nodded towards the radio, motioning for Charles to go ahead.

I clicked the radio and said, "This is Detective Charles."

Immediately, Charles turned and grabbed the cord, trying to pull the radio back. "Joey, what the fuck, man?"

"Relax a second," I said. Pushing down on the talk button again, I said, "Contact the New Jersey police. Have them send a squad car to Downing Homeless Shelter on Claremont Avenue, just west of Cavern Point Drive. You got that?"

The dispatcher on the other end replied, "Got it. Then what, Detective?"

"Have them ask for the director of the shelter. His name is Jimmy. I don't have a last name. Have Jimmy take the officers to where Edmonton Daniels is. Mr. Daniels is a key witness in an investigation. He's friendly. Take him into protective custody because his life may be in danger. Got it?"

"Got it, Detective. Making the call now," the voice came back.

I handed the radio back to Charles. "Thank you, guys. We're getting close. Lucy should be right—" I saw the lights of the ambulance and police car "—there."

Arriving at the scene, both Detectives Farnsworth and Charles identified themselves. Lucy's car was pretty banged up. She'd been hit on the left front side, and the front fender had caved in over her left tire.

I hurried to the back of the ambulance. "Is she all right?" I asked one paramedic.

"She lost consciousness a couple times, but she wouldn't budge until you got here, assuming you're Mancuso," the fellow responded.

"I'm Mancuso. Let me talk to her."

They opened the door. Lucy was lying on a gurney. Her head was covered with a bandage with blood by her ears. "Lucy, I'm here. We'll take care of everything, but you need to go to the hospital."

She grabbed my hand and squeezed it, and nodded in approval without saying a word. Just then, Harry arrived. "This is her husband, Mr. Roberts," I said.

"Jump in, sir. We'll be leaving now," said the paramedic.

I gave Harry a hug, and they took off. Farnsworth and Charles were waiting for me by Lucy's car, holding off the tow truck attendant who was in a hurry to tow the car away. I reached into the car and removed the key to open the trunk. All the while, I was hoping our evidence hadn't been removed.

I asked the tow truck driver, "Where's the other car?"

He looked at me, a bit confused. "What other car?"

"The car that caused the accident, a black SUV," I answered.

One of the police officers on the scene replied for him. "It was a hit-and-run, Detective," he replied, thinking I was with the NYPD.

"Did anybody see what kind of SUV it was?" I asked him.

"All I heard was that it was an SUV and black, no make or model," he replied.

My thought was that it might've been the same black Cadillac Escalade that ran Kathy down. "Let's open the trunk, Charles," I said, giving him the key. I wanted an NYPD Detective to take custody of our item.

Charles walked to the back of Lucy's car and popped the trunk open. We all looked at each other. "Is that it?" Charles said, pointing to the evidence.

I let out a big sigh of relief, saying, "That's it."

Wearing latex gloves, both Charles and Farnsworth removed the evidence and placed it in the trunk of their car.

We got back in the car. "Can I go with you guys and see that someone log this properly?"

"Joey, you've got to tell us what the hell is going on here," Charles said.

Farnsworth chimed in, "Does this have anything to do with the homeless guy that was killed last year?"

I was in a quandary. Someone knew what was going on. These guys had been tagging me for a few days, but the question was...why? "Let me ask you guys something," I said. "Why have you been on my ass for the last few days?"

They both eyed each other. Finally, Charles answered, "Joey, no matter what you think of us, the captain likes you and knows you have a nose for solving cases. The moment he got a call from the commissioner, he knew something was up. The fact is we've been tagging you 'cause the captain felt you were onto something, and he wanted us to help you when and if it became necessary."

Farnsworth added, "And here we are, making sure the chain of custody isn't broken with your evidence."

I didn't know if this was bullshit or if these guys were being honest with me. I was stuck with them. I gazed out of the window as Farnsworth drove to the precinct. I wasn't really focusing on anything I was seeing.

My cell phone vibrated. It was Marcy. "How's Lucy?"

"She's banged up. A concussion, probably, but I think she'll be fine."

"What about the item?" she asked.

"Under police protection. Are you still at the pub?"

"Father Dom and I are making calls like you asked. So far, everyone has agreed to come...reluctantly."

"Great. I'll be back after we lock this up at the precinct," I said. Then I remembered Edmonton. "Do me a favor, Marcy. Call the Director at Downing Homeless Shelter in Jersey. His name is Jimmy. Inquire about Mr. Daniels. This is important. Call me back after you speak to him. Thanks."

"What about Edmonton?" Marcy asked.

"I had Jersey Police detach a squad car to pick him up. I was concerned about his safety. If this hit-and-run was intentional, that means someone knows what we have, and his life could be in danger."

"Really, you think that?"

"I don't know. I just don't know."

"I'll find out his whereabouts," Marcy said as I disconnected my phone.

CHAPTER TWENTY-SIX

The scent of the detective squad hadn't changed. It was like I was home again. You could smell the food that lingered around various desks, from morning coffee to stale bagels and doughnuts. I hung around the precinct while Farnsworth and Charles logged the evidence. Greeting other detectives and friends that were in this morning. Everyone moved around doing their duties in the coordinated chaos that always existed in the room.

As Farnsworth and Charles walked out of the evidence room, my cell phone vibrated again. I was hoping it was news about Edmonton, but the caller ID read "Roberts."

"This is Mancuso," I answered.

"Joey, Harry here. Can you come over to NewYork-Presbyterian?"

"Of course, Harry, what's up? How's Lucy?"

"She's gone into a coma, but before she did, she kept saying your name."

"I'll be right over, Harry. Hang in there. She's going to be okay," I said, not really knowing if she would be.

I turned to the guys and asked, "Can you drop me off at NewYork-Presbyterian?"

Charles replied, "Of course, man, why?"

"Lucy is in a coma. Her husband would like me to be there."

"Let's go," Charles said. "Did you say hello to the captain?"

"Never got around to it. Maybe after. I appreciate this," I replied.

We took off in their car lights and sirens blaring again. Once there, I rushed to the emergency room as Farnsworth and Charles wished the best for Lucy.

I could see the long faces of Harry and his sons, Dean and Sammy, as I approached them in the waiting room. We hugged, and we exchanged few words.

I sat next to Harry. "How is she doing?"

"They found a brain aneurysm, but they're treating it. She's still in a coma."

"Anything else?"

"Just the concussion, nothing else, no."

"I know it's hard, but both are treatable. Where's Frank, your oldest son?"

"He's driving from White Plains. He should be here soon."

I wanted to make small talk but found it tough. "What's he doing in White Plains?"

"He's with IBM now. Great opportunity for him, and he's not that far from us."

"He's a bright boy. He'll go far in whatever he does," I said, not knowing what else to add. I patted his right knee as he sat back, and we both closed our eyes. People were moving around through the wide hallways with white tile floors. Patients were being scooted on gurneys every which way, and the all-too-familiar loudspeakers kept asking doctors to report somewhere. Hospitals had a rhythm and sound of their own. I hated that.

As I sat back, I went into a semi-conscious dream sleep that took me back to when the roles had been reversed...

***

Two years ago, Lucy and I responded to an active shooter, a 10-32, a person with a gun in upper Manhattan. We were first on the scene, and an Incident Commander hadn't been established yet. One of the various 9-1-1 calls said one shooter shot persons on the tenth floor of the building. The dispatcher informed us that the space was leased to a small company that was an online marketer of various electronic products. It was called Online Sales, and the shooter hadn't been identified.

Not waiting for backups, Lucy and I entered the building and took the elevator to the ninth floor. Our plan was to cautiously walk up the stairs to the location of the 10-32 or person with a gun.

Carefully, we entered the floor with me leading the effort and Lucy covering me from behind. Moans and screams could be heard from various offices, but doors were closed. As we attempted to enter some offices, we found doors locked.

As the incidence of these crimes have increased, many office buildings and companies have adopted protocols for occupants and employees in the event of such an occurrence. They have been taught to hide first, run second, and only as a last resort, fight. The locked doors we encountered were a response to rule one protocol. Yet, the moans and screams were still coming from inside some of these same locked offices.

Had the shooter been there already? Were people hurt? Was the shooter still in one of these offices? We had no way of knowing the location of the shooter unless he fired again. Something we were hoping would not occur. After what seemed like an eternity but was only a few minutes, we heard a man screaming in one office. We both approached. Carefully and quietly.

As I put my ear to the door, clearly, I could make out the voice of a man with a certain Asian accent. He was demanding to know where the owner of the company was hiding. From what I could hear, his demeanor was rapidly becoming agitated as he got louder and louder with his demand.

"I kill her if you don't tell," I heard him say. Based on that, I assumed that there must be two persons in this office besides the shooter. He was talking to one and threatening the second. Or, while others could be in the room, the "I kill her" could mean he was pointing his gun at a specific person, ignoring however many others could be present.

Not knowing how many victims are in a room and the location of the shooter is not an ideal situation for bursting into a room with guns ablaze. Calling to him could exacerbate the situation. From training, we know that in these events, the shooter has an acute awareness that he or she will not survive. They know that there are three choices, two of which lead to their likely death. Being shot at the scene or committing suicide are the most common, with being arrested a third but improbable result. Knowing that, the shooter is likely to cause the most damage as his or her imminent end nears.

The next thing we heard after his last loud demand was a shot and a scream. In a matter of seconds, I told Lucy I was going in and heard her say my name. I slammed into the door with my upper body and left shoulder leading the way. It all turned into a slow-motion movie, although things were happening at incredible speed. In movies, the hero breaks down the door, locates the perpetrator, and shoots them on the spot, saving the day.

But…I wasn't in a movie. I broke open the door but fell on top of it as my body kept going from the energy I had generated. Unlike a Hollywood scene, I saw the Asian man holding one pistol in each hand as I rolled on the floor. I remember his eyes opening wide with surprise. Before I recovered from my embarrassing entrance, I saw him lower the gun in his left hand, again in slow motion. I think I even saw the round as it left the barrel of his gun and traveled directly to my left hip. The pain that overtook me left me frozen on the floor.

In my peripheral vision, I saw a shadow over me and heard three rounds fired in rapid succession. My first thought was that the shooter was finishing me off, but I felt no more pain. The shadow was my partner, Lucy, as she entered the room and killed the perp on the spot with two shots to the head and one to the chest. He died before he even touched the ground.

The last thing I remember was the spoken word "ass." Later, Lucy told me she leaned down and said to me, "Wait 'til I tell the story of your entrance and falling on your ass, cowboy." We found out, subsequently, that the Asian man had been an employee who was fired a week before.

***

A few hours later, I awoke right here in this same place. One room to the left of where Lucy lay in a coma at this moment. My eyes opened, and I realized I'd fallen asleep on the chair. As I focused, I could see Frank, Harry's oldest son, embracing his dad and the two other brothers.

"I'm sorry, guys. I fell asleep."

"Nothing to worry about," said Frank, embracing me as I got up with a little smile.

I asked, "Good news?"

Harry turned to me and replied, "Nothing official yet, but one of the nurses inside Lucy's room gave us the thumbs-up through the window. We're hopeful."

CHAPTER TWENTY-SEVEN

Lucy was going to recover. The meds to combat the aneurysm were working, and she'd awakened from the coma. Only Harry could walk into her room and be with her for a few minutes. Her only response had been to smile at Harry, but that itself was a good sign.

Marcy arrived at the waiting room and embraced Harry's boys. Nodding for me to remove myself from the group, she said, "Edmonton is fine. Jimmy, the director of the shelter, had him taken to another shelter in Newark, and an officer stayed behind."

It relieved me. "That's good news. We don't need anyone else hurt because of this."

"I can't help but remember the last time I was here," Marcy began. "It was you that time. I thought you were…," she paused.

"I know. I just had a flashback to that event of a few moments ago."

"You lost so much blood. We were all concerned."

We were standing a few feet away from the waiting room. Looking at her face, I grabbed both her hands and asked, "Was that the moment you decided you needed more time to think about us?"

She remained quiet for a few seconds. Taking a deep breath, she said, "It was, Joey. Like I've said before, with Dad's death in 'Nam and then Alberto deployed in Iraq for a year, it was hell for Mom and me. I don't think I can live with the daily fear of losing you. You and I have seen too many of those stories."

"The good news is, I'm not in law enforcement anymore. I'm not risking my life every day."

"I need to know. Would you ever consider going back to law enforcement?"

So…that was her fear. Me going back to work as a detective. I said, "When I joined the NYPD sixteen years ago, I wanted to make a difference. In all honesty, it was that or becoming a part of my dad's life. It was being a part of righteousness or crime. I dedicated myself to be the best at what I was doing. Always with the goal of being a homicide detective. It bothered me and still does, to see innocent people die at the hands of others. You can say that my father taught me a lot of what not to do."

"So, it wasn't Father Dom that pushed you into the police force?"

"Dom had an enormous influence in my life. He may have been the catalyst or offered the guidance for me to see a better way of life. It always bothered me to see the injustices committed and the total lack of respect for life that some displayed around me when I was a kid. No, Father Dom didn't push me. He showed me a different way I could be a good person. That was something I was searching for myself."

"I understand. But I can't live with the fear that I might come home one day, and you won't come back from work."

"You still want to know if I would, assuming I even could, join a police force?"

"Yes."

I gazed into those beautiful green eyes of hers and knew she wouldn't be happy with my answer, but I had to be honest with her. "Marcy, I don't want to have to rule it out or make promises I may not keep. Who can say what the future holds for us? We're young. You can't define your future with certainty. You can plan and wish for something, but destiny is dealing the cards. The best we can do is to learn and be prepared to deal with the opportunities and the challenges dealt to us."

"It hurt me when you refused to take the medical disability offered to you then. You could've walked out with almost your entire salary as disability pay."

"Why would that hurt you?" I asked, somewhat confused.

"It showed me that your job was your number one priority, and I was second. You ignored my pleas back then, and that hurt me."

I could've turned that around about her own job. However, I've learned never to ask a question I don't already know the answer to. What if she said, "Yes, I'll give up my work for you anytime"? Then what? Instead, I embraced her and said softly, "I see it now, but I didn't see it then. I was selfish, but honestly, back then, I thought you were being selfish asking me to give up a career I loved. I'm sorry, Marcy. I love you."

"Thank you, that means a lot. I love you," she replied, pushing back a bit and kissing me gently on the lips.

I smiled. "Then. That settles it."

She let go of the embrace and stepped back, smiling. "Not so fast, cowboy. Let's finish this case. I may still get transferred to Siberia."

"The FBI has a field office there?"

"You know what I mean."

"I do, but you just might end up running the office here in New York if we put all these clues together."

"We'll see."

"Regardless, my clock is ticking," I said, laughing.

"Mancuso, your clock is just fine."

Frank walked over to us. "Joey, Dad says to come over. You can go in and see Mom now."

Lucy was alert and talking. She seemed weak yet was in good spirits. She flashed as big of a smile as she could muster when I walked in and waved me closer. "Is Edmonton okay?"

That was probably what she wanted to ask me before she went into a coma. "He is, Lucy. He's safe."

She smiled and closed her eyes, adding faintly, "Sorry about lunch Sunday."

"Hah, you have a rain check on the *moros.* We'll do it soon. Not a problem."

Marcy and I said our goodbyes to Harry and the boys. It was time for the family to be together, and we had to plan our reveal for Monday morning.

CHAPTER TWENTY-EIGHT
Sunday

I was stressing about the presentation on Monday. Sunday's break was perfect to plan and prepare. Marcy and I enjoyed a peaceful day in her apartment. In the evening, we headed back to the pub to help Mr. Pat and the staff close. I wanted to set up for Monday's whodunit game. Upon closing, we moved all the tables that covered the center of the establishment to the walls. We lined up the captain's chairs theater-style, with their backs facing the front door of the pub.

From last count, I knew we had a full house showing up. The five participants, or our suspects, had all agreed to come in. Some of them had said their attorneys would accompany them to this charade, as one called it. Also, we had law enforcement personnel who had been invited and agreed to take part. Albeit unwillingly. Finally, I had two more groups that comprised our humble team, including Agnes and a handful of surprise guests. Not that I have a flair for the dramatic, but it'd be fun to expose some of these folks in front of an audience.

We had worked hard to put all these clues together, and we'd uncovered a series of other potential wrongdoings along the way. Someone was guilty of a double murder, maybe more, and Joey Mancuso would not let innocent people die without exposing the perpetrators.

Jonathan Parker may have been guilty of a few things himself. After all, he wasn't without sin. But murder wasn't the way his life should have ended. I've noticed that there is a credit and a debit counter. There is a double-entry system in life. While my brother will tell you exactly who the Master Accountant is without hesitation, for us wishy-washy believers, all I can say is, *someone* is keeping score. Regardless of our position in life, the double-entry system works. Some call it *karma*. Jonathan Parker was a son to his parents and a husband to his wife. Perfect or imperfect, his life shouldn't have ended as abruptly as it did.

Kathy Miller, our Stella, was another innocent victim. She was in her twenties. Full of life with a young boyfriend ready to partake in a future they should have chosen together. Her righteousness and willingness to do the right thing cost her the ultimate sacrifice. I would not let her killer go free.

Last, there was John Doe. My unsolved murder in my last case on the force. Homelessness itself is a penalty brought about by circumstances, and probably sometimes, by choice. I don't know if the double-entry system had caught up with my John Doe. Perhaps it had, but it wasn't for another person to cash him out the way they did. Whatever the reason, my Mr. Doe was homeless. Whatever penalty he was paying was his to live with. This case could go cold. Thus, my indignation. My investigation became a cold case. Not because we couldn't find a perpetrator, but because of some political pressure. The lack of respect for his life by whoever closed his murder investigation was beyond my comprehension. This case was a bitter remembrance for me, and I'd carried that bitterness with me for over a year. I was excited to finally unveil Mr. Doe's killer.

As usual, I ended up at Marcy's for a quiet evening, some adult beverages, and a romantic night. My life was good, but it did not still fulfill me. I really felt that I'd found in Marcy my soul mate, and I didn't want to lose that opportunity. I've always heard that luck happens when opportunity meets preparation. I was prepared to do whatever, including giving up a chance to be in law enforcement again, if the opportunity to be with Marcy forever became a reality.

Of course, being the immature asshole that I am, I wanted to make the choice myself and not be told or asked to do it. I was having a hard time getting to sleep. I laid there talking to myself. Could I have my cake and eat it too? Was it workable to continue to work crime cases from a stool in our pub? Would Marcy finally come around and follow her heart?

Part Three
CHAPTER TWENTY-NINE
Monday—Six Days After the Murder

Morning came, and we were all full of anticipation. Would our suspects show up? We'd made a compelling case for them to do so without pointing fingers at anyone. They probably thought we were full of shit and that anything we had was nothing more than circumstantial evidence, if that. Their attorneys thought, hopefully, this was an opportunity to uncover any information that could be detrimental to their clients. Besides, at their hourly rate, they wouldn't mind spending a couple of hours at our whodunit game show.

We set the pub up like a small theater. We lined chairs up with five chairs in the front for our principal characters. A row of chairs followed them for their attorneys, if any. Behind that, we had more rows of chairs for our law enforcement guests. We uninvited any wits, or witnesses, thinking they'd be better not attending and exposing themselves at this point.

In the front, we set up a table with some items. Props that would be used during the presentation. Between this table and the chairs, we left room for me to make my presentation to our guests. Father Dom and Agnes would sit to the left side of the guests in a row of chairs that resembled a row of jurors. I had even set up a small white screen behind me on which I would project some pictures I wanted to show during our little game.

When I became active in the pub's management, I initiated the idea of having wide tin buckets packed with plenty of ice and inserting twelve to eighteen various brands of beer in them. These buckets with ice-cold beers could be self-served by our guests when the bar was open. They'd simply show our attendants the bottles, and it would go on their tabs. There was something about beers chilled with lots of ice that was enticing to me. It proved to be a great way to sell beer during the afternoons and evenings, especially in the summer. We'd gone as far as serving six beers in smaller buckets right at the customer's table. Everyone loved it. Today, we'd taken the buckets and filled them with bottles of water packed with lots of ice.

Mr. Pat volunteered to come in early and help us direct guests to their assigned seating. He was acting as our usher for the moment. Right after nine forty-five in the morning, individuals trickled in. Mr. Pat was asking everyone who he or she was and following our scripted seating plan. Sinatra's 'My Way' playing in the background was my way, pun intended, to rub it in slightly.

The first three that walked in were expensive, custom-made suits. I was standing in front with Father Dom, Agnes, and Marcy. Although Marcy didn't want it to look like they involved her in the game for fear of a reprimand.

I asked Marcy, "You know these suits?"

Facing them, she replied, "The grey pinstriped is Stevan Kapzoff, attorney for Evans and Albert. The other three, I guess, might be associates of the firm."

Every new person walking into the pub had to glance at all the black and white photos hanging from the walls. It was a trip down memory lane, particularly for the New Yorkers. I nodded to Mr. Pat to seat them in the second row. The three suits glanced around our pub with disdain. However, we heard their comments amongst themselves about the photos hanging on the walls. Kapzoff nodded to Marcy and then said something to his associates.

A couple of minutes later, Mr. Evans and Mr. Albert made their appearance. They ignored us and wanted to sit next to Kapzoff, but Patrick gently asked them to sit in the front. With their backs to us, they remained standing and spoke to their legal eagles, exchanging a little laughter and showing some arrogance.

More suits walked in. Four, as a matter of fact. This time, while the suits were expensive, they were off the rack. I recognized the district attorney for New York, the ADA, who'd worked with me in the homeless murder investigation of John Doe, and two other cohorts. They sat behind Kapzoff, and a little party broke out. Kapzoff et al., Evans, and Albert. Donors, donees, and intermediaries, I supposed.

Our mistress, model, and actress, Melody Wright, walked in by herself. She was sporting a mini skirt that I knew immediately would distract when I made my presentation. Mr. Evans seemed uncomfortable when he saw her walk in and said something to Albert in a hushed voice. Melody was all smiles. Totally ignoring Evans, she came over to the front to say hello to Dom and me. Dom then asked her to sit in the front row.

Our last two suspects walked in together with a third expensive custom suit. Mrs. Adelle Parker, a man I assumed was her father, Andrew Huffing, and what had to be their attorney. They acknowledged Evans and Albert but didn't seem friendly towards them. Mrs. Parker came over to us and introduced her father, but not the suit. I asked them to take their assigned seats.

Glancing at my watch, I saw it was five minutes to ten, and I said, "We'll get started in a few minutes. I'm expecting a couple of more people. Thank you."

Kapzoff said, "I assume you're Mr. Mancuso?"

I nodded and replied, "Yes, I am."

"Mr. Mancuso, be on notice that this charade of yours will more than likely result in a civil lawsuit against you, your brother, and anyone else involved in this outrageous game."

Father Dominic took a hard swallow. Marcy extricated herself from the front and walked towards the back of the chairs. I faced Mr. Kapzoff and replied, "Point taken, sir."

As if on cue, it was the DA's turn to apply a little heat. "Mr. Mancuso, I don't know what you have planned, but you'd better tread lightly, or there'll be more than a civil lawsuit following this little game of yours."

I turned to Father Dom, now sitting to the side. His face was turning white as pure snow. I smiled at Dominic. I wanted to say, 'Father, you're fighting the Powers of Darkness daily, and yet these two fellows intimidate you?' I faced the DA and said, "I understand, sir. Thank you for being here."

Finally, our last invited guests, the cheap suits, walked in together, my good friends Cagney and Lacey—make that Detectives Farnsworth and Charles—and Marcy's boss, Special Agent in Charge Victoria Stewart of the FBI's New York White-Collar Crime Division.

I was getting ready to start when the front door opened and in came my former partner, Detective Lucy, sitting in a wheelchair and aided by her husband, Harry. They both smiled and took a position at the back close to Marcy, who was sitting beside her boss.

I stood in front of our assembled guests, glanced around, and tried to make eye contact with everyone. There's always anxiety when you speak in front of a group. You can never get rid of the butterflies. The best you can do is to get the butterflies to fly in formation. However, when you are facing a group of panthers, tigers, and other ferocious wild animals ready to pounce on you, it takes added concentration.

"Thank you all for being here. Sorry we're running a few minutes late. I believe this presentation will be informative and prove fruitful for many of you. Let's begin.

CHAPTER THIRTY

"Ms. Melody Wright," I began, "thank you for being here."

"Oh, this seems like fun. Happy to be here, Joey," she replied, smiling and pulling her skirt down a bit.

"Good, I'm glad you're happy," I said as I noticed Mr. Evans moving in his chair uncomfortably.

"For those of you who don't know, Ms. Wright was born in San Diego."

Melody was surprised, and her smile turned into a frown.

I went on, "Anyway, she was born Susan Ashen, and at twenty-two, she became the close friend of a well-known Hollywood producer. She was following her quest to become an actress."

Melody interrupted me. "What are you doing?" she asked.

"I'm just introducing everyone to our guests," I replied, looking at her and then at my notes. "Mr. Wesland Scott, our Hollywood producer, divorced his wife of ten years. That's the marriage of ten years. Not Mrs. Scott," I said, facing the group. Thinking I was funny, but no one had as much as a smile on their faces. Tough crowd. I went on. "Immediately after his divorce, Mr. Scott, thinking Melody, make that Susan Ashen, was pregnant with his child, married Susan," I said, pointing at her. "That seemed the honorable thing to do. Unfortunately, Mr. Scott, twenty years older than his new bride, didn't get to see what he thought was a new son or daughter or even get to celebrate his first anniversary with his new young bride. Mr. Scott died of a drug overdose only six months into his new marriage."

I could see over my notes that Mr. Evans kept crossing and uncrossing his legs. However, Melody sat there stoically.

"Susan Ashen," I said, facing the crowd, "inherited a million dollars as stipulated in the prenuptial agreement with the balance of the inheritance going to Mr. Scott's children from his prior marriage."

I walked a little closer to Melody and asked, "Did you have the child?"

Moving in her seat and again pulling down her skirt, she replied softly, "I had a miscarriage."

All the way in the back, Farnsworth said, "We didn't hear that back here."

I raised my view towards the back of the room and said, "She said she had a miscarriage."

Farnsworth replied, "Sure."

Everyone turned back to Farnsworth.

"Let's go on. Suddenly, Susan Ashen, or Melody, vanishes from any public records. However, our researchers found our Melody about four years later in Silicon Valley with a new name. Suzanne McIntyre, who became Mrs. William Molden. Mr. Molden is still alive, and he was and is an innovator and creator of computer technology. Mr. Molden is extremely wealthy, despite having paid Suzanne a two-million-dollar settlement upon their divorce a year after their marriage. He continues to pay Mrs. Molden, our Melody, a substantial annual stipend."

I had the crowd's attention, finally. Only Melody and Mr. Evans seemed a bit troubled by the revelations.

I approached Melody again. "Any children with Mr. Molden?"

She just shook her head.

"That's a no, for you guys in the back," I said, glancing at Marcy, who was smiling back at me.

I flipped the page in my notebook and winked at Dom to my left. He gave me a nod. "So. what became of Suzanne McIntyre or Mrs. William Molden, you ask?" Making eye contact with the crowd, I continued, "She moved east. Right here to the Big Apple and hooked up with a Mr. Vittorio Agostino. Unfortunately, Mr. Agostino declined our invitation to join us today. More on Vittorio in a minute. Suzanne must have gotten tired of her name. You know how it is. I'm sure we all, at some point or another, would like to change our names, right? Anyway, Suzanne became Susan again. Only this time, she became Susan Osmond. There wasn't much on Susan Osmond. Other than her close relationship with Mr. Agostino. Mr. Agostino is one of the original investors in Evans, Albert, and Associates, a hedge fund company located two blocks from our building. Mr. Evans and Mr. Albert are here today, and I thank you for being here," I said, looking at both.

I saw Kapzoff touch Evans' shoulder and whisper something. Albert turned to Kapzoff and nodded.

"You're probably wondering when Susan Osmond became Melody Wright, right?" I said, wanting to be a smartass. "There's no trace of Melody Wright anywhere. Until last year, when she became a resident of the Upper West Side and leased an apartment at Riverside South. Just then, she became close friends," I coughed, "with Mr. Agostino. And we found out a company owned by Mr. Evans and Mr. Albert leases that apartment."

Kapzoff snapped, "What are you insinuating?"

"I'm sorry. Did I insinuate?" I replied, "Allow me to go on. None of these name changes by Ms. Wright were done in the traditional manner. All these names are new identities taken on by Melody," I said, glancing at her over my notes. "As a matter of fact, all the other identities are still active, and two of the names have offshore accounts in Panama—the country, not Panama City in Florida."

Sitting one seat away from Melody, Mrs. Parker asked, "How can you change identities so easily like that?"

I turned toward Adelle Parker. "Good question. You can buy what's called a 'three-pack' almost anywhere in the U.S. Particularly, in cities that have a high concentration of illegal residents. A three-pack can cost around three hundred dollars for which you will receive a driver's license, a passport, and of course, a Social Security card."

Melody got up from her chair. "I've had enough of this game," she said, starting to walk towards the back.

"Sit back on your chair, please," said Victoria, Marcy's boss.

"Who are you?" Melody asked, somewhat perturbed.

"Oh, that's FBI Special Agent in Charge Victoria Stewart."

Everyone turned back as Melody took her seat.

"Melody, do you own a Cadillac Escalade SUV?" I asked.

"I don't own any cars," she replied.

Mr. Evans became very uncomfortable and turned to his attorney, Kapzoff, saying something I could not hear.

"Did you rent a Cadillac Escalade?"

"No," she replied sternly.

It was time to begin the show-and-tell with my white screen. I nodded at Agnes. A picture of a black Cadillac Escalade flashed on the screen. Agnes oversaw the computer with the presentation we had prepared. The photo on the display showed an SUV with damage to the front.

"Do you recognize that SUV?" I asked, looking at Melody.

"No," she replied, without even raising her face to see the photo on the screen.

"Let me ask it this way. Did you, as Susan Ashen, rent that SUV from Enterprise Rent-A-Car this past Thursday?"

Kapzoff got up from his chair. "Ms. Wright, do not answer that question."

Melody looked back at him.

"That's expert advice, Melody. I would follow his suggestion," I added.

I nodded to Agnes, and a second photo appeared on the screen. The screen showed a picture of a California driver's license with a picture of Melody under the name of Susan Ashen. We followed it by a second scanned photo of the rental agreement signed by Ashen on Thursday, the day an SUV hit Kathy.

"Preliminary inspection of the SUV," I began, "shows clearly that it was involved in an accident and that there are traces of blood on the hood of the car. Once forensics examines the SUV, I am sure they'll show that the blood belongs to Kathy Miller, the victim of a hit-and-run accident on Thursday two blocks from here." I pointed at Farnsworth and Charles. I said, "Detectives?"

Both detectives got up from their chairs and walked over to Melody, cuffing her and walking towards the back.

Kapzoff said, "Our firm is representing Ms. Wright, and she is not to be questioned without us being present." Kapzoff dispatched one of his associates towards the back as Detective Charles began 'Mirandizing' Melody.

"There's more to this," Melody said loudly.

Her new attorney spoke to her and told her to be quiet.

"Detectives," I said, "stick around." They nodded and began making a call to a squad car to remove Melody, I assumed. I wanted Melody to stay, so I asked, "Detectives, would you mind if Ms. Melody stays with us until the end?"

Farnsworth replied, "No problem."

"Thank you," I replied.

I started my presentation again. "Coincidentally, Kathy Miller was an employee of Evans and Albert, but more on that later. Allow me to turn my attention to Mrs. Adelle Parker and her father, Mr. Andrew Huffing."

CHAPTER THIRTY-ONE

Another suit walked into the bar. Not an expensive suit, but off-the-rack stuff. Another civil servant, I assumed. The man spoke to FBI Special Agent Victoria, Marcy's boss. Victoria and the suit walked toward me. "Can we have a word in private, Mr. Mancuso?" Victoria asked.

"Of course," I replied. We moved back behind the white screen and away from the guests.

Victoria spoke in a hushed voice. "This is Special Agent William Casals with the FBI's Organized Crime Division in New York."

I nodded at Casals. "What can I do for you?" I asked.

Casals surveyed our surroundings to make sure no one was listening to us. "You spoke of Agostino, and Victoria called me immediately. We've had an ongoing agent undercover. They're embedded with a faked identity, looking into Agostino. What you're discussing today might jeopardize that body of work, and worse yet, out our undercover agent."

"I see you're referring to Katerina Rostova," I replied, taking a guess.

Casals' eyes met Victoria's. He looked back at me with consternation showing on his face. "I can't discuss it, and I'd appreciate it if you don't, either."

"Okay, I won't, Mr. Casals. Neither Agostino nor Rostova are an integral part of my revelations today. Fair enough?"

"Thank you. I owe you, Mr. Mancuso," Casals said, relieved at my quick acquiescence.

"Can I have that IOU in writing?" I asked, smiling at both.

Victoria grabbed my hand. "Joey, we won't forget. Thank you. Get back to your presentation. You're doing an outstanding job."

Casals shook my hand, and we walked out to the front. Both Victoria and Casals went to the back. I noticed it was a little more crowded with four uniforms standing in the doorway.

"Sorry about the interruption, folks. We were about to discuss Mrs. Adelle Parker, the widow of Mr. Jonathan Parker, who passed away last Tuesday." I noticed Adelle shift her position on her seat. Her father grabbed her hand and whispered something to her.

"Mrs. Parker is one of five persons who may have seen Mr. Parker last before he lost his life. Ms. Melody Wright, sitting in the back, is another. The other three are Mr. Huffing," I pointed to him, "and Mr. Evans and Mr. Albert. More on that later. Unfortunately, besides losing her husband, Mrs. Parker's finances have been significantly affected. Not only did she lose her husband's income. But they also tied the investments she made through him with Evans and Albert up in illiquid assets. The returns on those investments have been greatly diminished. Thus, her income from those has suffered." I saw tears in Mrs. Parker's eyes as she wiped them away.

Kapzoff, the attorney for Evans and Albert, was losing his patience. "Are we getting somewhere with this?" he blurted out.

I went on, "Mr. Parker had a life insurance policy of five hundred thousand dollars whose beneficiary is Mrs. Parker. Therefore, she's not entirely without means, albeit a trivial amount for some. However, a year ago, a new policy for two million dollars was issued on Mr. Parker's life. But there are two problems with that. One is the fact that the policy, in its first year, does not cover suicide as a cause of death. It seems they did the medical exam a month after the policy was signed. The effective date of the policy, or I should say the first anniversary of the policy, is two weeks away. The insurance company has declined to pay on the policy since they ruled the death a suicide. Here is the biggest problem with that policy. Mr. Jonathan Parker never signed the application for the policy. And the person who took the physical for the approval of the policy wasn't Mr. Parker."

Huffing snapped at me, "What the hell are you talking about?"

"Let me get to that," I replied, glancing at the back of the room. "A Mr. Robert Sands took the physical posing as Mr. Parker. Unfortunately, Mr. Sands could not attend this gathering. He was the General Manager of Andrew's Sporting Goods, a company owned and later sold by Mr. Huffing and his two daughters, Mrs. Parker being one of them. Mr. Sands has had a secret liaison for the last year with Mrs. Parker, as well."

Huffing turned to his daughter, Adelle, and asked, "Is this right?"

"Mrs. Parker," I said quickly, "I would not answer that. Handwriting experts have examined the insurance application and have concluded that you signed the documents. Not your husband. The PA, or physician's assistant, who performed the medical exam has agreed that it wasn't your husband that took the physical. The same PA identified Mr. Sands as the person he performed the exams on."

Huffing said, "This is preposterous. How do you know all this?"

"Mr. Parker suspected his wife, thinking that she was being unfaithful, and hired a private detective to follow her."

"He hired you?" Huffing asked as he pointed at me.

"No, that would've been too much of a coincidence. Although, I do have the private detective's report," I said, picking up a file from the table behind me. "Mr. Parker made a copy of it and handed it to his assistant, Kathy Miller, the young lady who was killed on Thursday. We could get a copy from Kathy's boyfriend. Mr. Parker feared for his life and handed his assistant a sealed envelope in the event something happened to him. A sort of insurance, pardon the pun."

Adelle Parker was in tears. I raised the file and saw Marcy. "Ms. Martinez," I began, as Marcy was already on her way to the front, "I think it's your turn to take Mrs. Parker to the back."

Marcy came to the front, cuffed Mrs. Parker, removing her to the back of the bar.

Huffing turned to Mr. Kapzoff and asked, "Can you handle another case?"

"Of course," Mr. Kapzoff replied, dispatching another associate to sit with Adelle in the back.

Kapzoff turned to me and asked, "So, did Mrs. Parker kill her husband?"

I made eye contact with him and then with the audience. "She had a motive, right? But stay with me. We'll get to that. I glanced at Andrew Huffing. "Mr. Huffing," I said, "Now let me address you."

CHAPTER THIRTY-TWO

"By the way, we have ice-cold water on the tables," I said. "However, if anyone wants an adult drink or a cigar, we can accommodate that, too."

The district attorney raised his hand. "I'll take you up on the adult beverage and a cigar," the DA said, asking Kapzoff if he wanted anything.

"Great, Mr. Pat can take care of you with that," I said, pointing at Patrick, as he got up from one of the side chairs next to Father Dom. "Anyone else? Feel free. It's on the house."

The uniforms grabbed bottled waters from the ice-packed buckets in the back. I waited a couple of minutes. Some had a need to use the restrooms, and others were taking advantage of the freebies Mr. Pat was handing out.

Marcy came up to me. "You're such a ham, Mancuso."

"Sweet ham, I hope. Is your boss happy with us now?" I asked Marcy.

"She loves you. I told her to wait for more surprises."

"Let's get back to business, folks," I said, asking everyone to take their seats. My last three suspects hadn't moved from their chairs. The DA was the last to sit. Raising his second Belvedere on the rocks, he thanked me for the beverage. I winked at him.

"Okay, let's go on," I said. "I have to thank my brother, Father Dominic. We started this investigation at his request. Mr. Parker had been a patron of our little establishment and visited us the night before his untimely death." Dom seemed excited at my recognition of him and smiled. "As you can see, he's not your typical Catholic priest. Sitting next to him is a young lady who has been instrumental in our investigation." Agnes smiled and waved at the crowd expecting applause, which wasn't forthcoming.

I began, "Mr. Huffing, you were one of the last persons to see Mr. Parker alive. Therefore, we had to include you in our research. We could not speak with you in the last few days. Your daughter, Adelle, told us you were in the Caribbean trying to free up some of the funds tied up in offshore certificates of deposits. Deposits made by Evans and Albert's company. It seems Mr. Parker persuaded you to invest the proceeds of the sale of your business, Andrew's Sporting Goods, after Parker joined Evans and Albert."

"That's right, but when I left his office, he was alive," Huffing said.

"We'll get to that, yes. I want to thank the FBI office in New York for allowing me to make this presentation before them acting on it, which they planned to do this morning."

Andrew Huffing looked back and saw a new group of attendees wearing blue windbreakers with large yellow FBI letters emblazoned on the back.

"Besides visiting the Caribbean Island of Bonaire, an excellent place for scuba diving...forgive me, I digress. You also visited Mexico City," I said, noticing Huffing uncrossing his legs and rubbing his forehead. "In Mexico City, you met with Señor Rafael Galan, who was the attorney that represented the consortium that purchased your sporting goods business a few years ago. Galan is also the attorney who represents Señor Ricardo Lindo. They alleged he runs the Lindo drug cartel in Mexico and California. Remember the name Robert Sands from a few minutes ago?" I asked and looked at Huffing. "Sir? Mr. Sands? The man who became your daughter's lover and partner in the insurance fraud was also your general manager and has been with you many years working at your stores."

Huffing could not take it. "Where do you think you're going with this?"

I ignored his question. Reviewing my notes, I proceeded, "Mr. Robert Sands is being held for another fraud case unrelated to this and has disclosed your entire scheme to launder funds for the Lindo cartel. They paid you twice as much for your stores than they were worth when you sold them. Forty million dollars, I believe, when, at most, the stores were worth twenty million. For years, you laundered drug funds through your store's cash sales. Mr. Sands has testified that you convinced Galan to invest Lindo's share in the Evans and Albert hedge fund, with Mr. Parker to add a further layer to the illicit money. The problem is that you just recently realized that the funds were illiquid, and Lindo was asking for his money. Money which you didn't have access to. So the proverbial shit hit the fan, and you were trying to buy time with Lindo."

Attorney Kapzoff reached over and touched Huffing on the shoulder. "We can help you, too."

Huffing glanced back angrily and stayed silent.

"To aggravate matters a bit more, each of your daughters were ten percent owners of your business. This morning, in Tallahassee, Florida, the FBI took your daughter, Anita, into custody."

"I did not involve my daughters in anything," Huffing said.

Legal eagle Kapzoff reached over to him. "Don't say another word."

I winked at Marcy. She was already walking towards the front. "Ms. Martinez, if you will," I said, nodding toward Huffing.

Marcy cuffed Andrew Huffing and sat him next to his daughter, Adelle, who had broken into another crying fit.

Kapzoff asked, "Are you almost done?"

"We're coming to the end. Although, I wouldn't complain if I were you. You picked up four new clients this morning," I said as the law enforcement crowd broke into laughter.

Evans and Albert sat there, subdued. They knew that their turn had come.

CHAPTER THIRTY-THREE

My front row was depleted. We had removed and cuffed three of my suspects in the Parker murder on other charges.

"We're almost done, folks," I said. "Mr. Evans, may I pick on you now?"

Robert Evans got up from his chair. "I've had enough of this," he said, turning to leave the room and seeing for the first time the number of law enforcement personnel in the back of the room.

Lucy, my former partner, who had been smiling all along and sitting in her wheelchair, cried out, "Sit your ass down."

Attorney Kapzoff stood, reached over to Evans, touched his shoulder, and pointed to the chair. "Rob, sit and don't say a fucking word. I've got this."

Uneasily, Evans returned to his seat and sat.

I started again. "My last case at the NYPD went unsolved. I ran into a lot of walls during my investigation. After that, I retired from the force—I'll leave it at that. But it bothered me that an innocent man lost his life, and we weren't able to bring his murderer to justice."

Evans turned to Kapzoff and whispered something.

"The case was a murder in an alley behind the 21 Club. An excellent restaurant, by the way. The victim was a homeless man, a John Doe. Mr. Doe's death resulted from being struck on his head by a blunt object. Earlier that evening, Mr. Doe and another homeless person witnessed an argument in the alley behind the 21 Club. Later that same night, our John Doe died in the same alley. By the way, the other witness identified Mr. Doe as Jimmy, so I'll use 'Jimmy' instead of 'John Doe.' Jimmy and the other witness identified the two men arguing in the alley as Mr. Robert Evans and U.S. congressional representative Horatio Stevens. Mr. Stevens was only a candidate."

Evans couldn't resist. "Those bums were drunk in the alley."

Kapzoff reached over. "Don't say another word."

"Besides the fact that Mr. Evans just admitted to being in the alley, we could confirm that Evans and congressional representative Stevens were patrons of the 21 Club that evening. Employees in the restaurant will testify that they saw both walk to the back of the club and into the alley. We don't know the reason for the argument between these two men, but that doesn't matter at this point. What we do know is that Mr. Horatio Stevens was one of the original investors in the company formed by Evans and Albert. Moving on, the second witness that had been AWOL since the incident came forward after all this time..."

Evans became restless in his chair. I nodded to Agnes to flash a photo on the screen behind me.

"The witness, call him 'Ed,' was in the alley when his buddy Jimmy was struck in the head with a piece of wood. The two by four you see on the screen. Ed never came forward for fear that the same outcome that befell his friend Jimmy would come his way. Ed saw our murderer hit Jimmy on the head. Ed followed our perp around a corner in the alley. He witnessed the perp dispose of the weapon in a trash bin. But Ed retrieved and kept the murder weapon all this time. That weapon is in police custody and has evidence of blood on both ends. On one end, once the forensics team does an analysis, we'll find Jimmy's blood. On the other end, there are specs of blood from the murderer who cut himself with splinters. I am sure that the blood will match the killer. Also, we have fingerprints the police have already matched to Mr. Robert Evans."

Evans raised both his hands in desperation.

"Detectives Farnsworth and Charles, if you'd be so kind," I said.

Lucy, my partner in this old case, chimed in, "Go get that asshole, boys."

We'd seen this scene three times before. 'The perp walk.' The detectives cuffed and moved Evans to the back. I waited a minute and went on.

"We can move on to Mr. Thomas Albert III," I said as Albert crossed his legs in front of me. "As much as both Evans and Albert want to hide it, their company is in dire financial straits. Our research shows that both have maxed their lines of credit, both personal and the firm's."

Attorney Kapzoff moved from the second row of seats and took a seat next to Albert in the front row.

"However, we uncovered our deceased Mr. Parker had realized that the hedge fund of Evans, Albert, and Associates was not only trading on insider information, it involved them in a Ponzi scheme, also defrauding their investors. For those interested in a little trivia, they credited Charles Ponzi with the name in the 1920s. The practice is simple. A firm promises investors an above-average return, and they pay these investors with additional money coming into the company from unsuspecting new investors. Our most recent case in New York would be Mr. Bernard Madoff."

Albert thundered, "You have no proof of that."

"Frankly, I'm not here to prove that case. I'll leave that to the authorities. However, the documents Mr. Parker left with his assistant, Kathy Miller, do show a chain of events and accounts in which they commingled clients' funds with company funds inappropriately. His notes tell us he brought this up to both Evans and Albert within the last month. This is because he feared that the infusion of two hundred million dollars from his new client was going to be misused. To quiet him down, they offered him a partnership in the firm. That he handed his assistant, Kathy, a file with this information shows he was still troubled by the arrangement and feared for his life."

I took a moment to let that sink in. Everyone was still waiting for the revelation of the person who took Mr. Parker's life. I raised my gaze towards the back. "Could you bring forward our cast of characters and remove the cuffs, please? They can have a seat here in the front again."

Reluctantly, the detectives and Marcy brought everyone to the front and removed their handcuffs. Farnsworth, Charles, and Marcy, plus a uniform, stayed to the side by the perps.

CHAPTER THIRTY-FOUR

Annoyed by my little game, Kapzoff asked, "Is this some off-Broadway play, Mr. Mancuso?"

I smiled and walked towards Kapzoff. "It seems that way, doesn't it? We have a cast of characters, love triangles, greed, mystery, and murders. Along with that, all plays have three acts. So now, we enter the third and final act," I said, glancing around at the audience.

"Something bothered me about the cause of death attributed to Mr. Parker. As we progressed in our investigation of the so-called suicide, all these other things that we have discussed came out. All five of you," I said, pointing at my front row, "seemed to have had the motive to kill Jonathan Parker. All of you pointed to others as having been last in Parker's office."

I walked over to Melody Wright. "Ms. Wright's motive could have been jealousy. Parker dumped her one day before going on holiday with her and was supposedly planning a wedding in Aspen for New Year's. Then we uncovered a secret liaison with Mr. Evans and a prior relationship with Vittorio Agostino when she called herself Susan Osmond. Agostino was one of the original investors of Evans and Albert's company. A little convoluted, right? Allegedly, Ms. Melody ran over and killed Kathy Miller," I said as Melody lowered her head.

"I can say more about that," Melody interjected.

I put my hand out, stopping her from going on. "There'll be time for you to tell your story. Now is not that time." I moved over to Mrs. Adelle Parker.

"Let me go on. Mrs. Parker was having an affair with Mr. Sands and may have had an idea her funds invested in the hedge fund were probably lost. So, she concocted an insurance fraud with her lover and was waiting until the policy was in effect."

"Mr. Huffing, her father," I began, taking a couple of steps towards him, "was also there the day of Parker's death and had a heated argument with Parker. He realized the money he had laundered for the Lindo cartel could be lost, and now he feared for his life."

Walking over to the partners seated by Kapzoff, the attorney, I stated, "The partners, as we have shown, had plenty of motive. If there was a Ponzi scheme and insider trading going on, that would have brought an end to their company, and they would face over one hundred years in jail...each. We know they were operating on fumes, as most of their money was gone."

The DA had been silent but smiling all along, enjoying his Belvedere vodkas on the rocks and a nice expensive cigar. Now, he asked, "So, who killed Parker?"

I moved to my table of props and removed a white sheet, uncovering five golf putters. I handed one to Ms. Melody, which she grabbed with her right hand. One to Mrs. Parker, who did the same thing, and one to Mr. Huffing, who followed suit and grabbed one. However, when I got to both Evans and Albert, neither one reached for the putter. They both ignored me and didn't grab it. I laid a putter between their opened legs, but neither one of them touched it. I then nodded to Agnes, and she flashed a photo of the same golf putter I had handed out to all five pictured on the screen.

"This," I said, "is a Scotty Cameron Tel3 Del Mar Two model golf putter. I assume you've all played miniature golf in your lives, so you know what this club is for. This model isn't readily available anymore. It's an old model. We searched Amazon, eBay, and other sites for us to find five identical putters. When I saw the body of Mr. Parker at the ME's office, we found a small blunt force trauma behind his head and above his right ear. It wasn't enough evidence for the ME to change his suicide conclusion, but we both felt that it could have been administered, the trauma that is, before the eventual death as he fell onto the landing on the second floor of the building."

I nodded to Agnes again. "Now, you see a picture of the putter's face, and if you turn it," Agnes flashed another picture, "you see that the front of the putter makes what seems like a right triangle."

I moved to the screen and, with my right index finger, pointed to the triangle. Both Melody and Mr. Huffing examined the putter they were holding. "This triangle fits exactly the puncture that Mr. Parker had on the back of his head above the right ear."

Albert wisecracked, "Good luck proving that. Parker was cremated."

Melody, Adelle, and Huffing turned to look at Albert.

I smiled. "I found it mysterious how Mr. Parker's golf bag was in his office on one day, and then the next day, it appeared at his home. Also, the large crystal Waterford ashtray and a golf trophy were sent to the home. Mrs. Parker confirmed that your office, Mr. Evans, had sent the items. You didn't send any other personal items Mr. Parker had in his office—pictures, artwork, etcetera. Only the three items mentioned. The golf bag, the Baccarat golf trophy, and the Waterford crystal ashtray. Our original thought was that one of these items could be the murder weapon. So, I stopped at your golf club in New Jersey, Mr. Albert. The same club Mr. Evans and Parker belong to. While asking questions, I was told that you have quite the temper. Few people like to play golf with you because of it. And you a have a reputation for throwing your clubs when you miss a shot." I said, pausing.

Albert's face became red and flushed with indignation. He got up from his chair, kicking the golf putter aside. From his jacket's inside pocket, he pulled out a snub-nosed .38 caliber revolver. There was a collective gasp from those sitting in the front, seeing the silver revolver aimed at me. I could see the rage in his face and his trembling right hand holding the gun as he took a step towards me. He pulled the trigger as I stepped to my left. For an instant, I had a flashback to when my dad was shot in Little Italy when I was a young boy. I had been there and distinctly remembered the day. I thought to myself, 'Am I going to die like my dad? From a gunshot wound?' The sound was deafening as the bullet grazed my right ear. Detective Farnsworth, who was standing in the front to the side, moved in quickly, grabbing Albert's right hand with both of his and kicked Albert in the groin. In the commotion, I heard someone scream out, "Joey," from the back of the room as the white screen behind me fell to the ground from the shot striking it. Within seconds, two uniforms reached the front. Together with Farnsworth, they wrestled Mr. Albert to the ground.

"Joey, are you alright?" Marcy asked, embracing me.

"I think so. Can't hear very well. Other than that, I'm good."

I glanced at the crowd. Everyone was standing. Evans was frozen in place. Kapzoff, his attorney, had a hand on Evans' shoulder. I wanted to go on, but I was a little dazed from the experience.

Dominic addressed the crowd, "Let's take five minutes."

The uniformed officers handcuffed Albert and sat him in the second row between them.

I walked over to Farnsworth and thanked him.

After a few minutes, everyone took their seats again. I stood up to continue.

"That was unexpected. I suppose we can add attempted murder to any other charges we may uncover. Right?" I said, smiling. Looking at Albert, "Let me go on. My assumption is, Mr. Albert, that on the day of Parker's murder, both you and Mr. Evans argued with him. Jonathan Parker could not go through with conspiring to hide the Ponzi scheme and the insider trading. The promise of a full partnership, if he kept his mouth shut, wasn't enough for him to be involved in the deceit and fraud you both created. Mr. Parker was a victim. Other than his misstep with Ms. Melody Wright, he was an honest person. We were curious why only three items were sent back to the home. Why lie about Mrs. Parker picking them up, and why only those three? Our assumption was that any of those items, the golf clubs, the Waterford ashtray, or the trophy, could have been the murder weapon. You, sir, in a fit of anger when you realized your scheme was over, took one of the golf clubs, the ashtray, or the trophy and struck Mr. Parker on the back of his head. Next, with the help of your cohort and partner in crime, Mr. Evans, you both pushed Jonathan Parker out the window."

Albert said, "Try using that in court."

"No, that will not do it, of course. But here is what might." That was the cue for Agnes to flash a new photo. A picture of a white rounded cast appeared on the screen. "Before the ME released the body of Parker for cremation, he made a cast of the back of Parker's head. The section that had the blunt force trauma. The mystery triangle. And guess what? After examining each golf club in the bag, fourteen of them, along with the ashtray and the trophy, we found one golf club, the Scotty Cameron putter, fit the blunt trauma, perfectly."

"That doesn't prove my clients did it," said Kapzoff.

"No, but remember, I was curious why the golf bag and the other two items, the trophy and the ashtray, appeared at the Parker residence the next day. Would it be possible to remove the murder weapon from the scene of the crime? And so, Detectives Farnsworth and Charles got a warrant, and they had the actual putter in Parker's golf bag dusted for prints," I replied.

Albert moved uncomfortably in his seat.

"It turns out that the only prints on the putter, anywhere on the putter, belong to Mr. Thomas Albert III. Before you say he could have used the putter in his office to practice on the carpet, the prints aren't consistent with the grip used when putting," I said as I grabbed a putter from Melody. "May I? Per the golf pros at your club who gave me a quick lesson on putting, this," I said, showing the grip on the putter, "is the standard grip when putting for right-handed persons. Which Mr. Parker, Evans, and yourself are. However, the prints on the putter are consistent with this grip," I said as I grabbed the putter in a manner compatible with striking someone. "I was further convinced just now that Melody, Adelle, and Mr. Huffing didn't use the putter to kill Parker. They had no fear of handling the putter I gave them. But neither you nor Mr. Evans wanted to touch the putter I gave you."

"Something else I found at your fancy club. Mr. Parker had stayed away from the club but played Sunday. Just two days before his murder. The protocol for caddies at your club is to wipe clean every member's clubs at the completion of the game. Otherwise, they can be fined. You guys are tough on these poor caddies. So, we know the clubs were cleaned, and besides, the only prints are yours, sir. Ms. Wright will testify that she saw you both walk out of Mr. Parker's office before she entered the office and found it empty and the window open. So, that makes you both the last to have seen Jonathan Parker alive."

Kapzoff whispered something to Albert.

I motioned to Agnes to turn off the screen. "That, folks, concludes our presentation." Farnsworth motioned to the uniforms to come forward. Now they, Marcy, and her boss Victoria were handcuffing the perps.

Melody asked a uniform if she could say something to me. He nodded, and she approached me, quietly saying, "Is this why you didn't want to have sex with me in your office the other day?"

"You were always a suspect, and I won't have a relationship with a suspect. I can't lose my objectivity, and I may, if I'm involved with a person," I replied.

She smiled. "I see."

"Let me ask you a question," I said to her.

"Go ahead."

"Is that why you wanted to have sex with me?"

"I found you attractive, but I thought that would help me."

"At least you're honest in that respect."

"What if," she paused, "what if I hadn't been a suspect? Would you?"

I smiled and looked into her eyes. "I'm already spoken for. By the way, if you want to make a deal with the DA, better get yourself another law firm. This law firm has their bread buttered by the partners."

"Yeah, but they're out of money. I'm not." Melody smiled and nodded as the uniform grabbed her arm and gently prodded her to walk towards the back.

She's not as dumb as she acts.

Before she walked back, she asked one more question, "What led you to my identities? My prints from the drink we had at Woody Allen's Booth?"

"No, we were late to get those after you qualified as a suspect," I replied.

"Then what?"

"Your kiss."

"My kiss?" she asked, as the uniformed police officer was getting eager to take her back.

"The napkin you left me last Monday with your name and number. You planted a kiss on it with your bright red lipstick as a signature."

"So, my lipstick was the clue?"

"No, not your lipstick. But we could rush a DNA test. From there, we uncovered your identity. Remember your first husband that died from an overdose? You were a suspect then, and your DNA was on file. After that, it was like dominoes falling. One thing led to another and another."

She smiled, "So I brought about this whole thing?"

I motioned to the officer to wait for another second and said to her, "Mr. Parker's death was the catalyst for our investigation. I think we would have solved his murder. Your involvement, however, led to a plethora of other crimes."

The DA asked, "Is the bar still open?"

I replied, "Yes, of course. Anyone that can stay is welcome to beverages." The DA smiled and walked over to Mr. Pat, who was behind the bar putting ice in some fresh glasses. I waved at Kapzoff, who was walking out with all his newfound clients. "We're having a wrap party for our off-Broadway play's closing night during happy hour tonight, and you're all welcome back then."

CHAPTER THIRTY-FIVE
Wednesday

It had been one day since our little off-Broadway play had closed. We'd been eagerly waiting for news on the crimes we uncovered. Marcy had come in early with *The New York Trib*, in which yours truly and Father Dom were featured on the front page. Marcy had sneaked a peek at the article, and she couldn't wait for me to read it. We sat at a table drinking *café con leches* she'd made.

"The article merits a victory cigar, Detective Mancuso. Can I light one up for you?" Marcy asked.

"Be my guest. You know I think women are sexy with a cigar."

"I wonder why. You're a sick puppy," she said, lighting up a Montecristo.

As she handed me the cigar, the sound of vehicular traffic signaled the front door had opened. In walked Mr. Pat, followed by a smiling Father Dom.

"I heard we made the papers," Dominic said. "Did you read the article yet?"

I replied, "Have not, Bro. Marcy did, but I've been waiting for you. Gather around. Let's read it. You too, Patrick. Join us."

I had the newspaper facing up on the table. On the left margin was a picture of the office building in which the offices of Evans and Albert were located. Right below that photo was a photograph of the front of our pub. Displayed prominently were our neon sign and logo, Captain O'Brian's Irish Pub and Cigar Bar. 'Dammit, that looks great,' I said to myself. I read the article:

"*Priest, ex-NYPD Detective lead cops to arrests*"
By Barry Simon, The New York Trib
"*Not since the arrest of Bernard Madoff in 2009 have New York authorities seen a Ponzi scheme and fraud of this magnitude. The investigation started by former NYPD Homicide Detective First Grade Joey Mancuso and his half-brother, Father Dominic O'Brian, from Saint Helen's Catholic Church in Brooklyn, on a hunch, led local authorities, the White-Collar Crime Division of NY's FBI office, and the Securities and Exchange Commission to multiple arrests for fraud and arraignments for three local murders.*

Mancuso and the Rev. O'Brian, licensed Private Investigators, began last Tuesday to ask questions about the suicide of Wall Street executive Jonathan Parker, who reportedly jumped to his death from his 21st-floor office window.

When asked why they began their investigation, Mancuso said, "The victim, Jonathan Parker, had been celebrating at our establishment the night before. My brother, Father Dominic, had spoken to him that evening and, upon hearing of the suicide the next day, found it odd that Parker would've taken his own life."

Mancuso and O'Brian started a series of questions from family and co-workers that led them to three murders and a slew of racketeering, money laundering, insider trading, securities fraud, and murder charges against five suspects. In a flair for the dramatic, the brothers invited the suspects to their pub, Captain's O'Brian's Pub and Cigar Bar in Manhattan's Financial District, together with law enforcement personnel this past Monday, and built a case against each of the suspects as they sat dumbfounded in the front row.

A witness at the proceedings called it "the best off-Broadway show of 2017." One by one, they handcuffed each suspect as the brothers made their individual case against them, removing them to the back of the room until the last revelation. It culminated in a Hollywood-style production, with all suspects holding a sample of the murder weapon, a golf putter, used to allegedly strike Parker and then push him out of the 21st-floor window.

I stopped reading for a second. Puffing on my cigar, I said, "Is that cool or what?"

Dom replied, "Great article so far; thank you for giving me credit."

"You started the chain of events. How could I not?" I said.

"Keep going. It gets even better," Marcy remarked.

I read on.

"Charged with the second-degree murder of Parker were Robert Evans and Albert Thomas, III. Both partners are owners of a Wall Street hedge fund, Evans, Albert, and Associates. Allegedly, Albert struck Parker on the head with a golf putter. Together, Evans and Albert pushed Parker out of the 21st-floor window of his office. The body came to rest on a second-story landing in front of the building and was discovered by passersby about an hour after the incident. Evans and Albert have pleaded innocent to the murder charge and are being represented by the law firm of Schultz and Essen.

To further complicate issues for the partners, a grand jury has recommended the indictment of Evans and Albert on charges of insider trading, creating a Ponzi scheme to defraud investors, and racketeering after a whistleblower came forward and presented evidence supporting the charges. If convicted, each partner could face over one hundred years in prison, not including possible conviction and sentencing on the second-degree murder charges.

They estimated the Ponzi scheme alone involved over thirty billion, much of which was used to pay new investors throughout the years and to support Evans and Albert's lavish lifestyles. Both men are well-known socialites in New York City and overgenerous donors to many local charities, as well as local, state, and national political parties.

In an unrelated case, the murder of a homeless person that occurred almost two years ago in the alley behind the 21 Club had gone cold. A witness, who had been in hiding and fearing for his life, came forward. Detective First Grade Lucy Roberts, then the partner of Mancuso, had investigated the case with him to a dead end. Roberts received a tip about the lost witness, located him, and put him under police protection.

The witness produced the murder weapon used to kill the homeless John Doe, identified now as Jimmy. A two-by-four piece of wood was used to strike Jimmy in the head and kill him. Blood on the wood matched the victim, Jimmy. Specs of blood on the opposite end of the wood are being examined and compared to that of Robert Evans. Latent prints found on the wood have already matched Evans.

Jimmy and the person who recently came forward witnessed Evans in a heated argument with a second man in the alley behind the 21 Club. Later that evening, Evans came back and killed Jimmy, evidently fearing he may have heard the argument. Evans later disposed of the murder weapon in an alley around the corner, stashing it in a trash bin. The witness followed Evans and retrieved the murder weapon, securing it all this time, hoping to develop enough courage to come forward, which he now has done. Evans has been charged with second-degree murder and has pleaded innocent."

I stopped reading, making eye contact with both Marcy and Dom, "Did you notice the congressional representative went unnamed?" I read on.

"A third suspect, Melody Wright, an aspiring actress and model, was charged with first-degree murder in the death of Kathy Miller, who was struck by a car in a hit-and-run on Thursday night as she walked on the sidewalk after leaving her office. Miller was the assistant to Parker, and both were employed at the hedge fund company of Evans and Albert. Police continue to investigate the possibility that Wright didn't act alone in the brutal killing of Miller.

Additional charges are pending against Wright, who allegedly has stolen and used various other identities to hide illicit offshore bank accounts under her various aliases. The law firm of Kapzoff and Associates is representing Wright. It is further believed that Wright is cooperating with authorities and may implicate Evans and Albert in the death of Miller."

I had to put down the paper and take a break. "Can you believe the Pandora's box we opened here?"

Father Dom was smiling. "It sounds more like a few boxes all at once, my goodness."

"Fellows, the phone has been ringing off the hook," added Mr. Pat.

I asked, "Who's calling?"

Patrick replied, "It's more like who is not calling. I've taken messages. You have local and national TV news producers calling. The AP and other news sources want an interview with you guys. There are invitations from cable news companies to appear on the morning shows. Even a well-known book publisher called with a potential deal. What do you want me to do?"

"We may have taken our little investigation business to a new level. Wow. Continue to take messages, Patrick. We'll decide later what to do," I replied. "I have a question, Marcy."

"About?"

"Arturo, Kathy's boyfriend. Isn't he in line for a reward if the Feds recover money from Evans and Albert?" I inquired.

She responded, "The SEC has a reward program for whistleblowers payable out of the Insurance Protection Plan that could pay him anywhere between ten to thirty percent of any money recovered. Although, he has a problem."

Father Dom seemed worried and asked, "What could that be?"

Marcy turned to Dominic and added, "He admitted to you that he had some involvement in the Ponzi scheme and knew about some of the insider-trading tips. Didn't he?"

"I remember nothing about that. Do you, Joey?" Dom asked, looking at me and shaking his head.

"I have no recollection of that, no."

"If he isn't implicated, it will entitle him to a reward. Plus, the IRS has another whistleblower reward system set up that might come into play."

We all gazed at each other and smiled.

Marcy went over to the front entrance. Eyeing up and down the street, she said, "There's a news van setting up shop across the street from your pub, boys."

I applauded. "Patrick, better get ready for a busy night."

Dom said, "Joey, let me read the rest. I need to get out of here, and I want to finish the story."

"Read on, Bro," I said.

"A fourth subject charged after Monday's revelations is Adelle Parker, wife of Jonathan Parker, the first victim. They charged Adelle Parker with insurance fraud and the attempted murder of her husband. Allegedly, Adelle Parker and a co-conspirator, Robert Sands, fraudulently took out an insurance policy on the life of Jonathan Parker, intending to kill him and collecting on the policy.

Sands, the lover of Adelle Parker, posed as her husband for the medical exam required for most new insurance policies. Sands, who is currently facing fraud charges on another case, is collaborating with authorities and has implicated Adelle Parker in the fraudulent insurance scheme. Kapzoff and Associates are representing Adelle Parker.

Finally, a fifth suspect has been arraigned on money laundering and racketeering charges. Andrew Huffing, father of Adelle Parker, is facing charges for his alleged conspiracy to launder funds for the Mexico and California Lindo drug cartel. Ricardo Lindo, a Mexican national, has been under investigation by federal authorities in the U.S. Lindo, the owner of a Mexican business consortium, reportedly bought Andrew's Sporting Goods stores from Andrew Huffing four years ago. Not only may he have overpaid for the business to launder funds, he was laundering illicit funds, also, with the help of Huffing, via cash sales for years, prior to Huffing's ultimate sale of the business to Lindo.

Sands was the general manager for the sporting goods stores, Andrew's, and has provided authorities with information on the alleged money laundering scheme.

I asked, "Anything else on the article?"

Dom replied, "No, just a little more blah, blah, and that the reporter will follow up with a full expose of all the persons charged with crimes. But we already know that part. Don't we?"

It obviously excited Patrick with all the commotion. "What do you guys want to do about the press and phone calls?"

"I'm sure as hell not in the mood to talk to any of them," I replied. "Father, you want to deal with them?"

"Oh, no. Not me," Dom replied. "I've got to get back to the church."

Marcy said, "Father, I can give you a ride back."

"I'm not staying here. Patrick, can you handle the bar?" I quipped.

"Of course, Joey, not the first time. Get out of here."

I turned to Marcy. "Dinner at your place?"

"If we order in, no problem," she responded.

I moved in closer to her and whispered, "Now that I'm famous, I want to talk about our future."

"Yeah, why don't you make love to me tonight, and we can talk tomorrow?"

"Sounds like a plan. I'll let you make the first move," I teased.

"Don't I always, Mancuso?"

Life is good.

EPILOGUE

None of the cases were immediately resolved. Justice is not necessarily swift. The crimes that Joey Mancuso and his half-brother, Father Dominic O'Brian, exposed that Monday morning at their pub took a little over a year to complete. All the attorneys worked ferociously on behalf of their clients.

Melody Wright was charged and found guilty of:

Aggravated identity theft, a class D felony in the state of New York.

First-degree felony murder for the brutal killing of Kathy Miller.

Money laundering because of using false identities to get the funds.

Tax evasion for failing to report the offshore accounts she held under her false identities and for failure to file a tax return for the same.

The prosecutors decided not to turn the case over to California, where Ms. Wright was facing additional charges for identity theft. While death is one penalty for first-degree murder and a Class A Felony in New York, the death penalty was negotiated to a life sentence in a plea bargain because of her cooperation with authorities regarding Evans and Albert and her pleading guilty. Melody Wright is serving a life sentence without the possibility of parole at Bedford Hills Correctional Facility for Women, a maximum-security prison in Bedford, New York. All her offshore accounts were identified and confiscated. They assessed her a fine of one million dollars, which she could not pay. Federal authorities continued to seek the cooperation of Melody Wright in connection with Vittorio Agostino, to no avail. Six months into her sentence, Ms. Wright was killed in prison, stabbed several times with a *shiv*—a crudely made knife. They have not solved her murder.

Mrs. Adelle Parker was charged and found guilty of:

Attempted murder, Class A Felony, because of her lover, Robert Sands' cooperation with authorities. Sands testified he and Adelle had planned to kill Jonathan Parker with poison to collect on the insurance policy.

Premeditated, planned, deliberate, hard insurance fraud.

Money laundering related to her father's ongoing laundering and the sale of Andrew's Sporting Goods.

Mrs. Parker was sentenced to twenty years at Bedford Hills Correctional Facility alongside Melody Wright.

Andrew Huffing was charged and found guilty of money laundering, again because of the testimony of Sands, who served in the capacity of general manager at Andrew's Sporting Goods since the inception of the business.

They sentenced Huffing to a five-year term at Lincoln Correctional Facility, a minimum-security prison facing Central Park in New York City on 110th Street. While the facility has a capacity of four hundred and six prisoners, it currently houses two hundred and seventy-five. The facility's neighbors include the Met and the Guggenheim, Museum Mile, and the Dakota Apartments, where John Lennon lived and when he was shot.

A year into his sentence, they broke Andrew Huffing out of prison. Mexican authorities found his body in Nogales, Mexico. They had shot him once in the back of the head. That crime remains unsolved.

Mrs. Anita Schilling, sister to Adelle Parker and daughter of Andrew Huffing, was successful in her trial. Her attorneys proved that Mrs. Schilling was neither privy to nor an active participant in the money laundering scheme concocted by her father. The authorities were successful in a clawback of two million dollars from her trust because of proving that part of the gains from the sale was from illicit profits. The clawback included an agreement to limit the amount to the two million or fifty percent, whichever was greater, of the amounts recovered from Evans and Albert's client invested funds.

Robert Evans was charged and found guilty of:

One count of first-degree Class A Felony murder for the killing of Jimmy, or John Doe, in the alley behind the 21 Club, and one count of second-degree Class A Felony murder for the killing of Jonathan Parker.

One count of conspiring to kill Kathy Miller, a felony murder.

Securities fraud and insider trading, because of Kathy Miller's boyfriend's testimony, even though the SEC had investigated the charges on a prior occasion and could not bring charges.

Operating a Ponzi scheme and defrauding investors. Again, the testimony and records brought by Miller's boyfriend, Arturo, were the smoking gun that sealed the case for the prosecutors.

Tax evasion.

Evans received two sentences of twenty-five years each for the murders of Jimmy and Jonathan Parker. Each sentence to be served separately, and ten years for conspiracy to commit murder. He received a sentence of twenty years for securities fraud and insider trading. Awaiting the completion of those eighty years in prison was a sentence of one hundred years for the charge of operating a Ponzi scheme. No further time was added for the tax evasion conviction. Evans was fined five million dollars and the forfeiture of his real estate properties. Mrs. Evans could keep two hundred thousand dollars and a small condominium in Albany, New York, as her personal residence.

Thomas Albert III was charged and found guilty of:

One count of first-degree Class A Felony murder for the killing of Jonathan Parker.

One count of conspiring to kill Kathy Miller.

One count of the attempted murder of Joey Mancuso.

Securities fraud and insider trading like Evans.

Operating a Ponzi scheme and defrauding investors, like Evans.

Tax evasion.

Albert is serving twenty-five years for the murder of Jonathan Parker, plus ten years for conspiring to commit murder. He will serve an additional twenty years for insider trading and securities fraud. Like Evans, an additional one-hundred-year sentence awaits him for operating a Ponzi scheme.

Two portfolio managers at Evans, Albert, and Associates were charged and found guilty of insider trading, securities fraud, and operating a Ponzi scheme. Both received fifty-year prison terms.

Both partners and their two portfolio managers are serving their time at the Clinton Correctional Facility in New York, which is the largest correctional facility in New York State.

Arturo Alvarez, Kathy Miller's boyfriend and an analyst at Evans and Albert, wasn't charged with any crimes. As a whistleblower, he may receive from the SEC's Insurance Protection Fund anywhere from ten to thirty percent of any funds recovered from Evans and Albert. It would take two years for the authorities to recover any funds. Arturo was to receive three million dollars. The IRS was in line to recover unpaid taxes from Evans and Albert, as well. Once collected, Arturo would receive an extra bounty from the IRS.

Edmonton Daniels, also known as Ed, was the second homeless person in the alley the day Evans murdered Jimmy. Ed would receive, as a gift, three hundred thousand dollars from Arturo Alvarez. With the funds and a government grant, Ed would open a homeless shelter in Harlem and become the director of the facility.

Joey Mancuso and Father Dominic O'Brian had been promised two hundred thousand dollars from Arturo Alvarez for solving the murder of Kathy Miller. The IRS awarded them a whistleblower informant award of fifteen percent of the taxes and penalties recovered from Ms. Melody Wright's offshore accounts.

The notoriety paid off before the money came in. Mancuso appeared on *Good Morning America*, *Fox and Friends*, and *The O'Reilly Factor* days after they filed the charges against the five suspects. The brothers are considering being consultants in a TV series offered to them by the cable channel USA. They continue to solve crimes from their headquarters, Captain O'Brian's Irish Pub & Cigar Bar in Manhattan's Financial District.

Agnes Smith received a bonus of twenty thousand dollars from Mancuso and O'Brian as a token of their appreciation for her hard work on this case. Agnes continues to attend early morning Mass at St. Helen's.

Patrick O'Sullivan, known as Mr. Pat, continues to manage the pub and has hired additional staff to handle some of his duties.

FBI Special Agent Marcela Martinez, known as Marcy, was offered a promotion to the Deputy Director of the FBI White-Collar Crime Division in Chicago, Illinois. Ms. Martinez declined the promotion and move, preferring instead to stay in the New York office, giving Joey hope that they soon will tie the knot.

—THE END—

—A note from Owen Parr

I trust you enjoyed reading A Murder on Wall Street. I certainly enjoyed writing and researching the material. While I tried to be accurate in police and legal procedures, I may have taken some liberties and made some errors, for which I am entirely responsible. This is a work of fiction.

A big Thank You always goes to my wife, Ingrid, for putting up with my aloofness during my writing. And to the many friends whose first names I have used for characters in the novel. Not everyone got equal billing, and I hope you forgive me for that.

The production and narration of this audiobook were done by Stefan Rudnicki of SkyBoat Media. If you like audiobooks, you'll love the work Stefan and his staff did on this one.

Other titles by Owen Parr

Operation Due Diligence. An Alpha Team Spy Thriller-Vol 1
Operation Black Swan. An Alpha Team Spy Thriller-Vol 2
Operation Raven—The Dead Have Secrets-An Alpha Team Spy Thriller-Vol 3
A Murder on Wall Street—A Joey Mancuso, Father O'Brian Crime Mystery–Vol 1
A Murder on Long Island—A Joey Mancuso, Father O'Brian Crime Mystery–Vol 2
The Manhattan Red Ribbon Killer—A Joey Mancuso, Father O'Brian Crime Mystery—Vol 3
The Case of the Antiquities Collector—A Joey Mancuso, Father O'Brian Crime Mystery—Vol 4
The Murder of Paolo Mancuso—A Joey Mancuso, Father O'Brian Crime Mystery—Vol 5
The Abduction of Patient Zero—A Joey Mancuso, Father O'Brian Crime Mystery—Vol 6
The Unsub—A Joey Mancuso, Father O'Brian Crime Mystery—Vol 7
THE Labyrinth—A Joey Mancuso, Father O'Brian Crime Mystery—Vol 8. (Release February 2021)
Jack Ryder Crime Mystery-Novellas 1, 2, & 3. The Case of the Dead Russian Spy, Murder Aboard a Cruise to Nowhere, Murder at the Beach Cove Hotel.
How to Sell, Manage Your Time, Overcome Fear of Rejection—A non-fiction, Self-Improvement Book

All titles are available at Amazon.com, BarnesandNoble.com, and other online retailers and as audiobooks at Audible.com